YOU WERE ALWAYS THERE...

'A Tale of Delusional Obsession'

DEVLEENA NAIK

BLUEROSE PUBLISHERS
India | U.K.

Copyright © Devleena Naik 2024

All rights reserved by author. No part of this publication may be reproduced, stored in a retrieval system or transmitted in any form or by any means, electronic, mechanical, photocopying, recording or otherwise, without the prior permission of the author. Although every precaution has been taken to verify the accuracy of the information contained herein, the publisher assume no responsibility for any errors or omissions. No liability is assumed for damages that may result from the use of information contained within.

BlueRose Publishers takes no responsibility for any damages, losses, or liabilities that may arise from the use or misuse of the information, products, or services provided in this publication.

For permissions requests or inquiries regarding this publication, please contact:

BLUEROSE PUBLISHERS
www.BlueRoseONE.com
info@bluerosepublishers.com
+91 8882 898 898
+4407342408967

ISBN: 978-93-6452-538-1

Cover design: Daksh
Typesetting: Tanya Raj Upadhyay

First Edition: November 2024

"In the loving memory of my Late Aunt Golanti Naik, I dedicate this book, like all life accomplishments to my parents…"
- Devleena Naik

This book contains subjects that might be sensitive to certain audiences. Kindly refer to the **Reader's Discretion (I)(II)** at the end of the book.

INTRODUCTION

'You Were Always There' is a story about Delusional Obsession of a young impressionable boy, who was deeply perplexed in 'love', set in an Indian suburban city. Growing up in a 'relatively' small town, we kids had always been sheltered from the mind games of people behind the glamour of the metropolitan cities. Suburban living was always peaceful yet restrictive, living in times where genders were attached with rigid social constructs.

Since childhood, we as girls weren't allowed to cross a radius of half a kilometre. Beyond that mark was no-man's land for us, and anyone who would see us outside of that, could potentially complain our parents that instant! After years of this conditioning, we found a way out of this adversity, growing up meant adventures and defying authority. It was a way of confronting our flaws and learning from failures. We would dream about being old and independent enough to step out, beyond any permissible limits. We would eagerly await the summer vacations as it was the only time we were free from the burdens of tests or any homework, and could focus on our hobbies. Funnily enough, our parents always expected us to complete the entire year's syllabus in the vacation's time only!

The place being bittersweet to us, had its demerits as well, people were quick to judge. The judgement being fairly unforgiving for women a little more. Many would believe that a girl, who dressed in tight clothes, laughed a lot while talking to boys, and walked across the street with her hair open, was seen as too "modern" or "progressive." And it wasn't always a good thing to be progressive, the word carried with it a negative connotation. However, the reverse as per convenience for a guy, was also true.

All my life, people around me disagreed to this on the face, but on the onset of any such circumstance, would not even shy away from sharing this very point of view.

Not much as a subject of taboo, but intersex friendships were generally not viewed very respectfully outside schools. Concepts of "dating and relationships" were rather termed as 'affairs', and all that families ever aimed for, was to get their children admitted to the top Engineering and Medical colleges *only*. Having spent the greatest part of life there, it's liberating to see people from my generation changing this firm mindset. Now parents acknowledge their children's decisions and share interest in their thought process.

Now, getting onto the "obsessive" part of the story; heartbreak and rejection are among the most sorrowful phases of human life. Everyone has gone through it at least once in their lifetime. Be it by the closest friend, sibling, partner or love. The sad reality is to accept it and move on. Some people do it by working on themselves, hitting the gym, getting a makeover; or picking up the pen and becoming a writer, the rest, play the guitar or hone any of their long-lost passions to keep themselves distracted from the reality that they now have to live with the fact that their love wasn't meant to be. Not because they were flawed, but because not everything can be rationaled.

Then there are those who "make-believe". They let the pride in their love take the better of them and convince themselves of a parallel reality where their love prospers because it is easier to live this way. However, this may take the shape of an unhealthy obsession, where the perpetrator tries to transmute their parallel, with the actual reality, leading to an extension of the made-up scenarios in their head.

Termed as 'Erotomania' in Clinical Psychology, and often caused upon the onset of trauma, this obsession when combined with the inability to accept rejection, takes a dark turn. The level of hatred that one faces because of this one-sided betrayal is unparalleled, where the perpetrator might even plot the downfall of the person he was once in 'love' with. Pop culture has also, time and again, validated this toxic trait, disguising stalking under the covers of 'deep passionate love', giving impressionable teens the worst idea of what true love is...

This story covers all these themes that might not be the appetite of a universal audience. **Reader discretion is advised.**

[This novel solely aims to entertain and educate its readers on the subject matters explored, not targeted to attack or defame anyone.]

Originally named 'Average Indian Whore', and changed due to creative differences, intended to call out the hypocritical nature we, as a society play in typecasting individuals and then behaving in ways with them that harms their self-worth and capabilities. A satire of how females become a victim of something that wasn't in their control in the first place...

PROLOGUE

"It's been raining cats and dogs for the past one hour and I had come to get the groceries on my bike. I try my hardest to escape the heavy pouring rain, but the raindrops on my specs are blinding my eyes. There's no choice but to wait out here in the rain! I park my bike at a shop's corner to remove my glasses, still standing by for the rain to stop. My myopic eyes blur my vision over again as I take them off to wipe it clean. As I wear them back again, I sense something eerily suspicious.

My fears grow loud as I look around. I bawl myself all over in a hasty manner, feeling the sounds of my breaths all over, I see no one...

I understand at once. It's him...

It couldn't be anyone else but him!

He who breathes in my shadows,

Follows me through the breeze,

Guards me like a canine...

Wherever I go, whatever I do, he's right there waiting for me...

He walks as I walk, and stops when I halt. There isn't a footprint of mine without his behind it.

My footsteps have lost their unique sound, they have become in sync with his!

It's weird, there's a sense of security even in my solitude, that I am never really alone. But the rest of the time, it feels just as haunting, because I Am Never Alone.

He is Always there. Everywhere...

But he never speaks, so what's the whole point of being around?

You could have been a friend?

But you're self-aware that way, you knew you were never worth me. So of all the times you asked, I turned you down! Warned you to never even try to get close to me; begged your friends to talk some sense into you, cried before your blood to spare me my life! But you turned to these petty ways, sniffing in all my steps. Investigating every human I ever laid my eyes on. Hoping I'd notice. But I have given up, given up yelling at you to be by your limits, 'cause you have none, none for me the least!

Back then, I used to fancy you for having a little more self-worth, but I guess, we're both way past that realization. Heaven may know what you get by all this! My friends would call you 'Delusional', but you no longer even feel like a snooper! You are my watchdog!

Not gonna lie, that one time I put my arm on Ron, I sensed you burning, enjoyed it even. Thinking like a juvenile, that it would make you never wanna see me again. But instead, you sent his private chats to his mother! Only to never be around any girl!

The raindrops lower; I take my bike and rush out... Just then, I see him come from behind the shop on his bicycle.

I smile to myself and leave...

TABLE OF CONTENTS

INTRODUCTION vii
PROLOGUE xi
CHAPTER 1: NEGATIVE BRAIN CELLS 1
CHAPTER 2: CHARACTER ASSASSINATION 45
CHAPTER 3: RUNAWAY DISGUISES 71
CHAPTER 4: F*D UP WORLD 88
CHAPTER 5: THE PLOT 102
CHAPTER 6: CLOSURE 129
EPILOGUE 149
CHARACTERS 151
DISCLAIMER: MENTAL HEALTH 153
ACKNOWLEDGEMENTS 159
NOTE FROM THE AUTHOR 161
SHARE YOUR LOVE 163
DISCLAIMER: READER'S DISCRETION 173

Chapter 1:
Negative Brain Cells

Valen: "And I THOUGHT YOU WERE DIFFERENT …"

"You have ended up being even worse than them!"

Summer (defending): "Why are you even listening to him? This is all a misunderstanding and he is the root of it all! Can't you see all this? He is literally smiling, he wants this between us! Why don't you trust me?"

Valen (heartbroken): "And let myself be hurt again? Sure!"

Summer: "Please don't talk to me like that! I haven't done anything to deserve all this. We can talk this all out, trust me!"

Valen (disappointed): "I did, Summer. I did… trust you more than anyone in the world, beyond what anyone said!"

(He was trying his best to keep his composure)

Summer: "No Valen, this isn't how it works!

(smirking sarcastically) This is really the moment when you should have given no damn about what people are saying! Did you even try to hear me out?"

Valen: "I can't do this, all your lies and manipulation. You can't just keep fooling me like always! I understand now; you pretend to be naïve and clueless when in reality, you understand everything differently..."

Summer (justifying): "See, I am not good with confrontations. It aches my chest and I palpitate! You don't know what I suffer from, then."

Valen (mocking): "How inconvenient, isn't it? Running away from the truth like it's so bothersome for Madame Samara."

Summer (tearing up, but still smiling): "How was it ever trust, Valen? When you were supposed to trust me, you fumbled. For you, great friendship is only for as long as you are having a great time, right? For when you need an escape and it's the happiest thing in the world?

One hardship, one hardship and you stumbled it all up!"

Valen: "You talk to me about trust? Then, why didn't you tell me about Reece?"

Summer (defending): "We don't have to do this, Valen. Don't bring Reece into this mess; this isn't really the right time to talk about him. I will tell you everything about him, I am not ready right now."

(The whole conversation was making me extremely anxious)

Valen: "Again, how bloody convenient? And this 'Pillar of High Esteem' was speaking of 'trust' and 'fumbling in friendships'? (tearing up) Trust me Summer, *of all the spineless people I've come across in my life, you are the one most hollow!* You have no foundation; forget about having a spine!"

There was silence... A painful bit of silence...

The world before me started crumbling, as my vision blurred and I found myself in the middle of nowhere. I was alone. I had never felt so humiliated and futile in my entire life. Of all the things that had ever affected me, started seeming like a bloody joke to me. He shouldn't have said that...

Summer (trembling): "I don't have anything to say. But I promise you, you are going to regret saying this all your damn life."

Valen (breaking down): 'Tell me honestly, did you ever get so close to him?'

Summer: "Valen, we need to talk about a lot of things before that!"

Valen (smirking): "We all laughed when we read those letters, what was all that?"

Aaron: "She is a wh*re, Valen. We all should have known all along! YOU HAVEN'T SEEN WHAT I SAW!"

2 years ago, 2018...

"Maybe it was the fragrance of your hair that doesn't let me sleep at night..."

"SUMMER, WHEN DID YOU GET SO CLOSE TO HIM THAT HE SMELLED YOU SO DISTINCTLY?" yelled my best friend, Ayo.

"That's something that even I want to know!!" I said, with my voice cracking and my heart pounding. There was a part of me that was laughing uncontrollably and another, that was scared to the gut...

"I guess that's something we should dig in deep!" Valen smirked.

...

4 years ago, 2016...

The name is Samara, Samara Laine. My friends call me Summer.

It began at that sick hour; I was 15, unapologetic and brainless...

We were at Avasa's place. Avasa was the 'it' girl of the school. But for us, she was this crazy little lad; raw, grounded, and ever-so-playful. She was a natural; every boy in school would die to talk to her, let alone be her friend. Our meeting had been long overdue!

Two of my best friends, Cherika and Ayona (Cher and Ayo, for me), had come with me to her place. We had made it mandatory to meet her once every summer. Avasa lived far from my house (approximately) one kilometre away! My mom would never let me go there alone, so I made Cher and Ayo her friends too. The three of us could now cycle our way to her house once every vacation!

We had just finished our End Term Exams for 9th grade. It meant no school, no homework, and no extra classes. We were living the best days of our lives! Avasa's mother was a warm old lady, determined to feed us unhealthy carbs to death that day! We had all the time in the world to chill by ourselves and could have fun guilt-free, till 7:30 pm! Our parents were treating us like grown-ups now. They wouldn't even ask where we went after 6:30 pm and we wouldn't be scolded for roaming around. I knew they were making quite the progress...

Avasa's brother Danish was the exact opposite of her, high on arrogance and testosterone. Mean, grumpy, and your typical know-it-all of sorts! He was just two years older than her, but I never understood how he was even remotely related to her and also Valen's nicest friend!?

Valen Moore; Valen was my best friend! He was a joyous creature and his charisma made everyone love him! He loved playing the class clown. Somehow, Cher and Ayo despised Valen. They would never mind me hanging out with him. To be safe, I never left them alone. It was a fatal combination, and I could not afford to shed tears for any of these pieces of heart!

We were all having a great time together at Avasa's place, we had even constructed a tent in her garden, playing cards as Danish burst himself into the lawn. Oh, I hated him so much; I could hit him any instant.

"You girls should do some real shit," Danish chuckled.

The good part was that all of us despised him equally, so we monotonously ignored him like a fly on the wall and continued our play.

Danish (interrupting): "We are so much better than you guys; you all are so stupid for making a house inside a house! Get out in the sun, dude, and play some real thing. I've come back after playing football!"

I turned around and was about to begin arguing as Ayo held my shoulder and gestured for me to stop. I turned back and continued to play the cards.

Danish: "Oh, see. Someone is triggered... (mocking) But Summer, aren't you a sweet little girl? You shouldn't be angry."

My blood boiled with every word that he uttered.

Avasa (yelling): "Shut up and leave, Danish."

Danish (continued mocking): "Why? Or else Summer would bite me?"

Cher (warning): "Watch your words, Danish, it's Samara for you. Only we get to call her Summer; mind your tongue or I'll punch you in the face."

Danish: "I'm so sorry, Cher. Did I hurt you too? Don't worry, Summer wouldn't mind me calling her that! Isn't she the sweetest girl to ever exist? You guys are so lucky to even be friends with her!"

Summer: "Danish, get the hell out of here or I'll break your bones!"

I was accompanied by the howling dogs around the street, echoing with my thunderous blow at him.

Her mom came running towards us to inquire what had happened.

Avasa (complaining): "Mom, ask this moron to be by his limits and stay away from my friends!"

She complained to her, explaining our little interaction with Danish.

Enraged and annoyed, Avasa's mom pulled Danish by his right ear and took him inside their house. Danish looked at me, grieving. As his mother dragged him through the house, he screamed smirking, "You'll know very soon what I mean, Samara...!"

He had always been a weird-bothersome guy, but today how he behaved was plainly mannerless. We played till dawn; then I came back home and crashed onto the bed. I was still thinking about what Danish had said. Why had he spoken so derogatorily to me? I couldn't remember doing him any harm, at least in my faintest memory. I couldn't comprehend any of this so I logged onto Facebook and texted Valen.

Summer: "You know what? The weirdest thing happened to me today?"

Valen: "What?"

Summer: "Your best friend Danish? He was behaving oddly with me and he called me 'the sweetest girl' over and over again."

Valen (casually): "Oh? I know what it's about."

Summer (curious): "Tell me?"

Valen: "So, the other day, we went to play football on this new ground beside the marketplace. We met a guy there who said you were his girlfriend!!! The funny thing is, we never even asked! Then I told him you were my best friend; I would know if it was true!"

Summer: "Exactly, I would have told you!"

Valen: "I don't remember his name, but it started with 'a' or 'b'; can't remember."

Valen: "Funnily, when we asked him why he liked you, he said that you're "the sweetest girl" he had ever seen..."

I couldn't hold it anymore, and burst out laughing! All my life I had been called a bully by my friends, the thought of someone thinking I was sweet was way too much for me to handle! A part of me believed it to be a prank, the other part was extremely curious to know more...

I asked Valen to meet me again in school as our new academic year was around the corner. I jumped over to my cell and immediately called Cher and Ayo...

Summer (screaming): "You guys know what? I have got spice to share!!!"

Cher: "Bee, Tell us already!"

Summer: "A guy likes me! And he thinks that I AM SWEET! I just spoke to Valen."

Cher (coldly): "If Valen said this, I'm sure this is a prank!"

Ayo: "Sweet? Wait, isn't this what Danish meant when he spoke to you like that?"

Summer: "Yeah, dude. Valen and Danish were together when they got to know about it. We need to find out who it is..."

Cher: "Shouldn't we just let Valen clarify?"

Summer: "I did, but he doesn't remember. He said his name starts with either the letter 'a' or 'b'."

Ayo: "That's so stupid, how would we ever know who this is...? Have we met him before? Is he someone we know?"

Summer (chuckling): "I told you all that I know, he just said he finds me sweet. This is the funniest thing I have ever heard from any living person! Nobody finds me sweet! He must be someone I haven't spoken much to."

Ayo: "That should be pretty easy! It can't be somebody from your batch! You have had feuds with all the boys in class, probably!"

Summer: "You're right, it cannot be anyone from my batch, and I don't interact with many senior or junior batches!"

Cher: "Valen and Danish are just playing with you. That's it. There's no point putting our heads into this so much..."

Summer: "Yeah, you're right. Why even engage our brain cells when we have no leads? By the way, did you guys watch the exclusive insight of the royal wedding?"

We carried on with our little catch-up ahead and spoke endlessly like we literally had nothing to do in the world...

Ayona Kain;

Ayona and I had known each other since I was 5. She was a petite, pale-skinned girl, high on adrenaline, with beautifully curled hair. She was a lovable-hyperactive creature, who loved participating in all co-curricular activities in school, be it drama, singing, debates and even sports like basketball. Often caught up being the people pleaser, she had the kindest heart. We became friends when my dad and her mom introduced us to each other and claimed to be each other's friends already. She lived right across from my house; we met each other every evening and would walk around the locality.

Cherika Shiki had been my friend fairly recently, but she was the sort who could kill for you any day (figuratively). I began calling her *Cher* since I was such a fan of the pop-queen, and we'd play her songs in the evening and dance to them! I met her at a painting class I'd go to on weekends. Our painting coach would always be enraged because we would constantly chatter during his class. He glared at us all the time but we would take up the same assignment just to be around each other. She soon became the sole reason I still went there. I loved painting and poetry, and so we found a match in each other!

Cher was a brunette, bold and unforgiving; radical in conviction and short-tempered. But she was also my protector who would go around spying every guy who ever approached me. She would often interrogate them for deeming themselves worthy. Being raw and brutally honest, her approval had been the most significant part of our decision-making. She disapproved of Valen from the get-go but only agreed for me to be his friend after persistent pestering.

The three of us were way more than just friends; we were sisters through thick and thin. We laughed, we fought, we hated each other for many things. But that never changed our sacred bond!

Valen and I became friends rather randomly; we would greet each other around the corridors. I mean, everybody knew everybody back in school. He wasn't my classmate, but our friendship was inexplicable. We never realized when those random conversations made us trust each other enough to share our secrets!

Valen was a six-feet-something guy, with puberty-hit stubble. He always loved being around people and making them laugh; he had an energy about him that was passionate and genuine, (something Cher never agreed upon) and I loved to be around!

One day, he tagged me on a Facebook post that said,

'If I ain't got you, then I ain't got nobody at all,' with 10 others, I was sure that we had become the closest of friends! Standard 10th was around the corner, and I couldn't wait to know more about my secret admirer. It was a strange feeling but these butterflies wanted to be fed upon!

3 days later...

We joined back to school after 8 weeks. I was caught up in my classes during the first half, so I waited till the lunch break to meet Valen. As soon as the bells rang for recess, I hopped out of my class with Ayo to meet Valen. He was with his boy gang. I called him out, but he wouldn't listen. I went to the other side to see him, where he was with his friend.

"I need to talk to you!!" I screamed amidst the chaos.

His friend glanced at me to ask who I was...

"I'm Samara. Valen's friend," I exclaimed, almost screaming.

"Wait, isn't she the one?" he tried whispering to Valen, as he nodded back at him.

I heard him, pretty clearly. I felt offended by the very tone of their interaction. I could feel the mockery in the air. I climbed down to leave and asked Ayo to follow me back...

Valen jumped before me and held my shoulder. "Wait, Summer, where are you going?"

Summer: "Don't you understand? Who is this guy spreading rumours about me? You are my only friend who knows this, but not helping at all!? I'm the butt of your jokes, first Danish and then this guy..."

Valen: "I am so sorry, Summer. But you seriously don't need to mind all this so much! People are going to have fun around; you see three weeks from now, nobody will even remember!"

Summer: "Then why don't you just tell me who it is...? At least I can go up to him and punch him in the face for spreading this petty rumour!"

Valen: "I told you I don't know his name, but I can explain what I remember. He must be in Standard Eight now, speccy, short-hair, skinny, nerdy, kinda looks like a toad..."

Summer: "You think this is a joke? What kind of a description is this?"

Ayo (speculating): "Standard Eight, wears glasses, looks like a toad, and his name starts with the letter 'a.'

Summer, if it is who I think it is, then we are in great trouble…"

Summer: "Who???" (I was growing impatient…)

Ayo: "My neighbour, Aaron!??"

Summer: "What? That's the stupidest thing I've ever heard! He's a kid; and more like a brother to me. It can't be him!"

Valen: "Yes!!! That's it! Aaron. That's the name!"

Summer: "This is no playtime, Valen; you have done me no good today…"

Valen: "No, Summer, why don't you get it? That's exactly him; does he play football?"

Ayo: "Yeah, all the time; he is such a bother when I try to study…"

Valen: "Does he also play the guitar?"

Ayo: "Yes, he does. Bad though, but he is ticking the boxes…"

I hear their senseless conversation and fall in the corridor kneeling, shocked!

Summer: "Guys, STOP. He is a kid… I always saw him as a younger brother if I ever did, there's no other reason to not be sweet to a kid!"

Ayo: "Dude, this is so messed up. We're in so much trouble! We have got to get him to stop all this!"

Summer: "Who all know about this, Valen?"

Valen: "Technically, every guy who plays football on the same ground. We only went there like twice, and everybody seemed to know it. There were guys from high school, even our older brothers from college."

(I start panicking, thinking about the number of people who believe in this bullcrap. They must be thinking that I'm of his 'sort'!)

(The bells ring again, the lunch break is over...)

Summer: "Dude, we're getting late, but we'll have to do something about this! Meet me later, Valen..."

We dash back to our classes and I wave him a distant goodbye.

...

Aaron Shaw

Aaron was Ayo's immediate neighbour who lived right across from my house. (Ayo and I lived diagonally opposite each other.) He was this nerdy kid, extremely arrogant and two years younger to me. I hadn't ever noticed him because why would I? He was socially an outcast. He did not have many friends in school to extract information from, but he was a part of a huge football gang. Despite being unaware of who these 'football' guys were, I was afraid that they would associate me with him. I did not want that.

I could hardly ever remember interacting with him.

There was this one time when I missed my van on the way back home, and had to come home walking. My mom would scold me if I asked her to pick me up. Our school was just around a kilometre away from home and Aaron would commute on his bicycle. He saw me passing by and stepped in to give me company on my way back home. It was indeed a sweet gesture, but not great enough of the gravity of "liking someone."

Since I was a kid, we celebrated the grand festivals together in the neighbourhood. But, with every passing year, more families moved out and the fun faded. This one year, it was technically just me and Ayo, but she also had to leave early to study for some exams. I was alone and was looking for people around to play with, when Aaron came in.

We would pass by each other a few times in the streets and I would smile at him as a pleasantry. I couldn't think of another scenario that could, rationally, invoke any feelings of infatuation towards me or anyone. Also, someone being attracted to me? Wasn't that extremely hilarious?

Anyway, I was sure this was less about him and more about his hormones, so I mightn't be too worried about it, after all!

...

[As decided, I meet Valen after school at the parking lot with people rushing out from everywhere.]

Valen (excited): "I have an idea! What if I become friends with him and bring in all the information?"

Summer: "Weren't you the one who told him that I was your best friend? Why would he tell you anything?"

Valen: "On a scale of 1 to 10, how much do you think he would remember that?"

Summer (mocking): "Not a lot. And I wasn't ever gonna say this... but you have brains!!?? How is that even possible?"

(Valen glared at me as I chuckled)

Valen: "I will make him a friend and ask him to spill all about 'his crush'. I'll pretend to not have paid much heed the first time. But when he tells me it's you, I'll give him the hope of setting him up with you as you're my best friend and in the process, also discover whether *he is worthy of you!*"

I knew he was provoking me; his face said it! As always, he wanted to irritate me with his mockery, but this time I had planned a little play-along.

Summer: "You're right! What if he actually is my knight in shining armour?"

Valen looked rather disgusted by it, I was loving it!

We laughed our way and left for home.

Later that night, he pinged me that he met Aaron at the ground and grabbed a lot of information. I was excited to know about my little admirer!

...

The next day...

Valen (worried): "So, we have a situation..."

Summer: "What do you mean?" (I was already scared of any news)

Valen: "Basically, the whole football gang, mostly his batch, know you as his (voice cracking) *girlfriend*. But the good news is, the other seniors find him too inconsequential to care. He said he met you two years back and you have beautifully long hair, gleaming eyes and your honesty made him fall in love with you..."

(I was shocked)

Summer: "What!??? That's ridiculous! Have they ever even seen me around him to believe in his bullcrap!? Why is he spreading such lies?"

Valen: "Dude, why are you overreacting!? Calm down. These are just rumours. Don't you know a thing about rumours? They aren't true. People talk crap about me all the damn time! Like not even kidding! 'Valen is double dating', 'Valen's ex-girlfriend found him cheating in the girl's lavatory', what not! You needn't bother about them so much! They have no basis and apart from his pocket gang, no one even cares. You shouldn't either!"

[I wasn't on the same page with him; he wouldn't ever understand where I was coming from! I realized, telling him anything would be about dragging on the same thing over and over again!]

Summer (speculating): "And why exactly did he tell you all this so openly? I mean, you guys have spoken just twice..."

Valen: "You have no idea about my superpowers, Doll. You'll see within a week; he will spill every detail to me himself!"

He was right; Valen was very manipulative. I knew his ways. He'd gather up all the information by hyping up something to someone, then trading the hype, some petty affair for something he wanted to know. He'd share a small update, then walk away with exactly the info he needed in the first place. I knew him pretty well because I had been a culprit of his sly ways.

One of the reasons why Cher disliked him was because she always felt he had layers and couldn't be trusted. He wouldn't even shed himself before someone he called a friend. She had major loyalty issues with him, and I couldn't blame her either!

A few days later, I saw Valen outside my house as I was dressing up for my coaching. I completely freaked out, my mother wouldn't be happy to see him there. I pretended to leave early for class! Right then, I saw Aaron coming out of his house and jump onto Valen's bike...

"Well, that was something...," I told myself!

What Valen said was coming true! Despite Aaron being an introvert, they were getting along too well. He hadn't come there to see me, instead, to pick him up for their little catch-up...

This went on for a few weeks where I'd catch them hanging around together. Laughing like they were the greatest of friends, Valen came over to pick him up from his home, and I'd encounter them in the hip hangout spots. Valen had unconsciously began ignoring me even while passing by!

I wasn't really too sure of this union. A part of me was actually insecure about them being such good friends. I had always tried to keep my friendship with Valen private because I hated any rumours about me.

But keeping everything aside, how could I ever tell Valen that I liked him all along...?

.

.

.

One of the reasons Cher despised him because she never really approved him for me. A part of me was aware of all his flaws, watching him play his games with people. None of that really mattered, for it was me, him, and our friendship—that's it!

But I could sense the chaos we were getting into.

Aaron liked me; I liked Valen, Valen thought of me as a friend, and Valen and Aaron were good friends!

Was I going to lose him in the game I let him start...?

...

After 3 weeks of barely speaking with each other, Valen called me up. He asked me to meet him after school. He was too excited to speak, I could barely make out his words through his screams over the phone.

Valen: "I need you to meet me right now, Summer. I have gotten the biggest breakthrough in the case!"

Heaven knew what case he was referring to. It was high in the afternoon; my mum would scold me if I left my house at this hour. He insisted and just landed in front of my house. I called up Ayo, who would usually be home with her nanny during the day, and asked if we could come there. I hopped into my slippers and ran down to her place.

Valen: "Dude, that guy is truly, madly, and deeply in love with you. He wrote two poems for you and insisted on giving them when I told him you were a friend!"

He pulled out two handwritten notes in all caps. They had a bunch of silly spelling mistakes. My heart was fluttering. Somebody had written a poem for me for the first time!

(passing me down the notes)

Summer (chuckling): "I don't want to read it! I'll laugh!"

Ayo (hesitant): "Give it to me! Let me read."

Ayo began reading as we dissected every line, word by word.

Poem 1: My Love for You

My heart beats for you; in every plight,
I can't get you off my mind; you're always in sight.
In the depths of the heart, a fire burns bright,
Maybe it's the fragrance of your hair,
that doesn't let me sleep at night!

This love, so pure and raw,
leaves me helpless, unable to draw.
I am unable to think of a reason, logic, or sense;
my mind is a roller coaster, and my emotions are intense.

I long for your touch, your embrace, your kiss.
Without your presence, I'm aching for your bliss.
But this craving can never be true—my only salvation is moving past you.

Poem 2: Forever I must wait

A love that transcends space and time,
A love, that is, truly sublime.
I'm trapped in this cycle of yearning and pain,
hoping against hope that your heart, I may gain.

I can't help but hope, can't help but dream,
that one day you'll see me as more than it may seem.
It lifts me up, sets my spirit free;
this love, my eternal destiny.

Sadly, I know it's just a fantasy
that your love for me can never truly be.
I'll wait for you, forever if I must
because in you my heart has placed its trust.

So let this love forever grow,
a love that the world will always know...

"Maybe it's the fragrance of your hair that doesn't let me sleep at night!"

"SUMMER, WHEN DID YOU GET SO CLOSE TO HIM THAT HE SMELLED YOU SO DISTINCTLY?" yelled Ayo.

"That's something that even I want to know!!" I said, with my voice cracking and my heart pounding. There was a part of me that was laughing uncontrollably and the other was scared to the gut. I did not know how to comprehend all this. Was it fair for me to laugh at anyone's feelings for me? But I clearly did not reciprocate with anything that was mentioned in these letters...

"I guess that's something we should dig in deep!" Valen smirked.

Strangely, the tone of his poems sounded as if, we already were a thing.

Ayo: "Don't you guys think he is in some serious trouble? Because according to this, you are *already* his girlfriend."

Valen (squeaking): "That's exactly what he has been telling people! He is even not approaching you anymore; you are in for some other level sh*t! I'm sure in his dreams you guys would have even made babies!"

I knew he intended to tease and annoy me, but my head was on a separate tangent now. He was firmly living in his made-up world. But what concerned me the most was that he was convincing the people around him to believe in all this too!

Our interactions could be finger-counted. And certainly, this isn't how someone feels about 'Love at First Sight' cause its one-sided. He never confessed to me anything in real time. I became so enraged that even the sight of those sheets of paper was maddening to me!

Valen could see my face growing tense, "What happened to you now, Summer? I was just joking, no need to get so serious about it! Don't worry, we'll fix this guy!"

Summer: "Just the way you were trying to fix me up with him!? Weren't you the one who said that these are just petty rumours? Just go give these stupid poems back to your best friend!"

Valen (offended): "Best friend? Seriously? I am doing all this for you Summer, to get him to speak and you are giving me this? Do you understand how insufferable he is to be around? He lacks the brain cells to even barely converse with, and I have to pretend to be good to him! My friends get so mad at me for not spending time with them and instead going around with him. I hear from them every day for being 'distasteful', just for you, and I get this from you?"

I had nothing to say! Like the rest of his friends, I was convinced that he was getting closer to Aaron! I was surprised by the lengths Valen was going to for all this.

Summer (trying to lighten up the mood): "Really? Well then, like your friends I also thought you had lost your taste for people to hang around with!"

Ayo: "Now if you guys are done with your little reunion, we have some real problem here...?"

Valen: "You know what? You guys think about what to do; I have some other business to attend to. We have to go beat up this gang at The Banyan Tree! I'll take my leave, my ladies..."

Summer (passing him the letters): "Take these with you and throw them on his face."

He left with the letters.

Ayo: "What's the Banyan Tree?"

Summer (squeaking): "It's an old tree in the middle of the marketplace where guys fight over petty conflicts. It has good traction for letting people know and notice them for being the Alpha!"

(We both laughed at the crazy doings of these school boys aspiring-to-be-men, but then came back to the subject at hand!)

Ayo: "What do we do with this guy? Trust me, it was all fun and games until I read this! I thought he just had a crush on you! And why have you involved Valen in all this? Don't you think he'll eventually know about your feelings?"

Summer: "I do not care about my feelings right now, and I do not even plan to share them with him! That will ruin our friendship! But this Aaron guy needs to stop!"

Ayo: "Should we talk to his brother?"

Summer: "Don't be crazy! That would be really embarrassing for him. He just likes me! The way I like Valen, telling his family about it would be unfair!"

Ayo: "But we should if he ever hurts you, right?"

Summer: "That's too extreme! But we'll think of something, babe! Don't worry."

Later in the evening, I came back from my coaching and was lying on the bed, tired. Valen called me up to meet. I was too tired to get out of my bed, but that wasn't ever his concern as he was already halfway there! I got up and jumped outside in my PJs; where he was waiting for me with his brother, Jude. Jude was Aaron's classmate. I asked why he wanted to meet me, to which he said, 'JFF: Just for fun!'

Aaron was outside his house and saw us talking...

Jude confirmed that Aaron had told his batchmates to not even as little as glance at me as I was supposedly *his*. The bare sound of these words coming together to form a sentence made me puke. He also mentioned how Aaron wasn't well-adjusted for society!

Valen, nevertheless, had his own agenda that day.

He stood closer to me deliberately and began speaking to me out loud, occasionally patting my back, holding my hand, and moving my chin. I had been friends with him for a long time now; he was doing all this just to tease Aaron. We saw Aaron get inside his house and shut all the doors and windows with a loud bang!

We continued our little catch-up, laughing endlessly as we spoke!

After an hour or so, Aaron came out of his house, enraged, and started shouting at us, "Can't you all keep it down!? Do you have any manners to behave!? My parents have sent me to tell you all to go! You are a menace to us."

Summer (interrupting): "Dude, they have come to meet me, and we're talking!"

Aaron: "You be quiet; you're the most mannerless and have the least sense of behaviour."

Valen (to Aaron): "Take your ass away from here right now before I slap you to death, and I promise we won't be a bother anymore."

His words were sincere, Valen was cold-blooded when it came to any of his friends. He immediately left with a rather disgusted face. I felt humiliated by the way he had spoken to me. Valen could make out by the look on my face.

Valen: "Come with us, let's grab ice cream!"

Summer (smiling awkwardly): "I guess I'm good, and I should leave too; my mom would be mad at me for staying out this late!"

We all left from there, but he had sensed my malaise, he texted me on his way back.

"He is an asshole and doesn't know how to talk to a girl; don't mind what he said. You are better than this!"

I did not want to put a lot of my head into this. I smiled at his text and went off to sleep.

...

A few days later...

As I was leaving for school, Aaron walked up to me, I tried ignoring him initially but he stepped in to stop me.

Aaron: "I'm sorry for that day; I shouldn't have spoken to you in that manner..."

(Honestly, it did bother me for a few days, but I no longer cared.)

Summer: "It's all okay, just forget it! I'm fine now."

Aaron: "Does it mean you forgave me?"

Summer: "Yeah dude, we're good, don't bother!"

Aaron: "Can you meet me today? I need to talk to you..."

Summer (hesitant): "Yeah, ping in the interval, I'll speak with you if I'm not busy!"

He grinned at the response and dashed away.

During recess, I was giggling around with my friends when he came to meet me; I let him come inside our circle.

"I need to speak with you," he said.

"Yaa, go ahead," I responded...

"ALONE...!" he declared.

I gestured my friends, and we left from there, walking around the corridors.

Aaron: "I shouldn't have behaved with you the way I did that day!"

Summer: "Yeah, you shouldn't have, but it's fine, dude. We're good. It's been a while since then, and I don't think about it anymore!"

Aaron: "You don't understand! I really love you, Summer! And that day when I saw you laughing with that stupid Valen guy, I couldn't hold back. I couldn't help but think about you, and I am sorry about it!"

Summer: "It's okay, I heard you; you don't have to repeat it over and over! And Valen is both a friend to you and I. Can you drop the 'stupid part'? Is there anything else that you wanna talk about?"

Aaron: "I love you, Summer. I really do."

Summer: "Yeah! I get that! If there's nothing else, can I go now?"

His expression changed rapidly, and I left from there. I could see him standing at the same spot when I reached my class.

...

The next day...

He walked up to me again during recess; I was chattering with my friends.

Aaron: "I need to talk alone..."

There was an awkward silence.

My friends started teasing him.

"Why do you have to talk to her alone *only?*" my friends squeaked, as we went out to talk. I could see them following us behind.

Aaron (with a disgusted look on his face): "You know, I have a medical condition where I shouldn't face the sun. Yet, I'd sit beside my window every Tuesday, Thursday, and Saturday at 4 p.m. to get a glimpse of you. It's the time that you leave for your classes, right?"

I was feeling a little violated by how he walked up to me. I wasn't interested in whatever he was saying; I just could not remember granting him any authority. Besides, he also had a track of my schedule.

Aaron: "My parents thought I was no longer interested in studying. When, in fact, I would be waiting around for you. I really love you, Summer. I don't know if you understand what I am trying to say!"

(My friends were still behind us, occasionally attempting to eavesdrop.)

Summer: "I get it, Aaron. Is this the only thing you wanted to talk about?"

Aaron (confused): 'Yes? I mean...'

"Also, your friends are really annoying! They see me around anywhere in the school and giggle among themselves!"

(I was getting impatient by everything at that point...)

Summer: "Dare, you speak ill of my friends! Yesterday, you said things about Valen and now these guys? If there's nothing else you want to talk about, then I have to leave now..."

Aaron: "Will you play football with me in the evening? You don't have your classes today!"

I walked away without saying anything.

Later that afternoon. Two girls from my batch walked up to me hilariously curious: 'Was he your boyfriend?'

'NO!' I exclaimed. I was getting extremely irritable.

With a desperate grin on their faces, "You can tell us; we won't tell anyone!"

Summer: "No, seriously, he isn't!"

They tried extracting gossip from me but walked back in disbelief. This was insane, these girls had been in my batch forever, and they would casually pass by me every day. Never had they walked out of their way to ask me about anything, my health, my academic performance, my scores or just anything about my life! Because I was with this certain someone, they took the effort to walk up to me to ask if I was dating that person.

In what world was that rational? I left from there terribly annoyed.

Later that evening, Aaron came to my place to ask if I would play football with him. Ayo and Cher were not at home, I couldn't disagree. We went outside to play. And he would strike up a conversation here and there. Initially, I was annoyed by how he had behaved with me that morning, but I eventually started enjoying the game. He showed off his moves as I struggled to even keep up!

I had a good time as we played for an hour or so when my mom called me back home.

...

The next day...

Valen: "You played the ball with him!"

(He came to meet me after school.)

Summer (casually): "Yeah, I did! I wanted to learn the ball! And I was free anyway."

Valen: "Are you ef'n crazy? He is now convinced of your little relationship."

Summer: "That's just baseless. He confessed and asked me about his love twice. I'm sure he would have understood that I rejected it, didn't reply to him, never will!"

Valen: "Then why are you giving him mixed signals? Are you interested in him? Tell me."

Summer: "Are you crazy? Why, in the whole wide world, would I be interested in him?"

Valen: "You tell him you don't like him but then also hang out with this huge smile on your face! Don't you understand that he would feel that there's a spark that he just needs to ignite? You're giving him false hopes that he might have a chance. With your actions, God may know if you would."

Summer: "I laugh, smiling around everyone! Does it mean I am interested in each one of them? I smile while talking to my gardener; does it mean that I am hinting something?"

Valen: "Are you seriously this dumb or just acting like it, Summer? Do you realize that nobody in the world, especially a girl, has ever spoken to him with respect? Back then, all your smiling at him was enough to put him under the impression that you were interested in him. Playing football would likely mean you were asking for something from him. All things aside, if you really wanted to play football, why didn't you ever ask me? I would have taught you in a week. You've been acting really petty lately, deliberately leading him on. What's going on with you, Summer?"

Summer (defending): "But you never offered to let me play with you!"

Valen: "Please don't say a thing that's more senseless than this. I don't want to think low of you, ever in my life. Give yourself some time to assess the situation and what you want. Else none of us, Ayo, Cher or I, will be able to help you."

Summer (exclaiming): "I know what I want!"

I honestly felt attacked by this. What did he mean, I was letting him feel this way.

Valen: "Tell yourself, and not me, if it's more than just validation..."

I was speechless.

.

.

.

Was he right? Why was I doing this? I could easily ignore him, but I chose to be nice to him. Well, for the record, he had been the first guy to ever take the patience to chase me so passionately. I had no feelings for him at all, but was I actually enjoying my moment of this harmless attention? Valen was right somewhere, even I did not know what I wanted from our little interaction.

A few days later...

Valen and I would often go to school together, Aaron had measured the time of our arrival. He would normally commute from a different route, but that day he came from our route to catch us going. Our classes commenced at 7 in the morning. Around 6:50 am, he came as we were walking and pushed his way between us. He was extremely high on energy and said random things as we walked.

We entered a narrow pathway on the way to our class, and he suddenly leaned against me sideways, pushing me in, his body almost isolating me into a corner. It all happened at the split of seconds, I did not understand how to react. Valen grabbed him by his neck and pushed away.

Valen (yelling): "What do you think you're doing?". He was burning with rage.

He said something abruptly, brushing himself off.

My heartbeat instantaneously shot up! Valen held him by his collar and jerked him off to leave.

Valen: "Why didn't you slap him?"

Summer (heavily breathing): "I didn't understand how it happened. I couldn't comprehend what I should have done."

Valen: "A guy was forcing himself on you and you didn't understand? Any other girl would have slapped him there. Do you still not understand what your "normally smiling" and "playing football" has done to his feelings? Get some brain that's a bit more conscious and aware, Summer! I cannot be there to always protect you!"

I actually should have slapped him...

I was super violated, but I did not. Was it my cowardice?

Valen had been so bothered by all this that he dropped me off at my class and dashed away immediately. We would usually talk till our teachers came by, but not today...

Later during recess, another girl saw me walking past the corridors. We danced together for a function once. She came up to me and asked if Aaron and I had been seeing each other. I was getting furious with all these rumours. It instantly reminded me of what Valen had said. I decided to never see him again, even if it meant being rude and arrogant!

...

One week later...

Valen and I met on the weekend. I told him that I had been completely ignoring Aaron ever since the incident. He casually murmured that he had *fixed* him.

"What?" I exclaimed! I couldn't decipher his words.

Valen: "Oh nothing. He was mannerless and needed some desperate fixing; I did that!"

Summer (irritated): "Will you tell me what happened, or blatantly play around your word games?"

Valen: "It's nothing; I have dealt with guys like him before! They think the world revolves around them!"

Summer: "Are you going to tell me or not?"

Valen: "Trust me, sweetie. He came up to me one day, and I showed him his place!"

Summer: "I'm leaving..."

Valen: "Oh God, why are you so stubborn!? He came up to my class one random day after that incident, I was chilling with my friends and he mumbled something. I thought he wanted to talk. I walked up to him and he asked me to (finger gesturing in the air) "stay away from you", warning that if he ever saw me around you, he'd end me or something. I punched him before he could finish his sentence! He was too entitled. I did not like him; he stood back up to say something, and I smacked him again! The first punch was for his audacity to walk into my class. The second was for mistreating you and whatever else he wanted to say by "warning me"! Poor thing, I accidentally broke his specs; the second one was a little too hard for him!"

Summer (surprised): "What?????? Firstly, will you stop making things sound so casual when they're not?!!"

Valen: "You think a lot, bub. He is not worth your time! Ignore him like a fly on the wall and that would be the real heartbreak. He lost his only chance to even be a friend and that's on him, nobody else."

Summer: "And when were you going to tell me all this?"

Valen: 'Whenever we were gonna meet next. Today! See, I told you!'

Summer (confessing): "You were right, I led him on! He always got the wrong idea about all this. I thought I was being generous to him!"

Valen: "Exactly, that's the problem! You haven't been sweet or generous to me, or your other friends. Why were you doing it with him then, knowing well after reading those letters how delusional he is?"

Summer: "I did not think of it like that!"

Valen: "Stop acting stupid, Summer. You most definitely don't like him! You usually have time for nobody. You have denied meeting me so many times; why did you not turn him down? Wouldn't have been difficult for you. It wasn't football; don't give me that crap! Then, did you enjoy the attention?"

Summer: "What are you even saying? What kind of girl do you think I am?"

To be honest, I was offended. The fact he was right, did not mean he could say crap about everything now.

Valen (leaving): "I'm here for you. I wouldn't want to sabotage our friendship for such a petty guy. Think about it peacefully; maybe you'll know then..."

Summer: "But how did he dare to even come near you? This is maddening."

Valen left from there, without saying a word... I called up Ayo and Cher for an emergency meeting and told them everything. I needed to be around somebody.

Ayo: "Babygirl, we should inform Brother Avi. He is pretty strict with him and the only person who can control him. Remember the last time we saw him speaking some crap; Avi glared at him once, and he shut his mouth! He is the only one who can help us and we need to stop this guy! Otherwise, he'll keep throwing off your reputation!"

Summer: "You're right. He shouldn't have involved my friends..."

Cher: "And Valen has come up and told us about this. What about the others whom he would have said something and we don't know at all!"

Summer: "But what do we tell him?"

Ayo: "EVERYTHING!" Ayo was firm.

Cher: "Yeah, tell him everything. He'll understand and give the right advice, even the right scolding you need, just admit the things that you have done wrong; otherwise, it would be unfair to him!"

Summer: "Yeah, I'll be honest! But are you guys sure that we should do this!?"

Ayo: "We cannot hold him back, Summer. He'll explode with every move, and you have seen his potential!"

They were right; I couldn't contain him anymore...

-end of chapter-

Chapter 2:
Character Assassination

Cher, Ayo, and I hung around every evening, and we often met Brother Avi to exchange pleasantries.

We planned to catch him that day, it was foolproof. Ayo would start a chat with him to set the tone of the conversation, and then I'd jump off and spill his brother's advances! I wanted to involve Valen in this too, but I was sure these girls would be displeased. We met that evening and waited eagerly for Brother Avi, but to our surprise, he was busy, and we had to postpone the plan.

The next day, he was working again. Ayo was growing impatient, so she abruptly marched inside his house to call him, as our only chance that Aaron wasn't home this time.

And he actually came out! It was totally uncalled, my pulse rate suddenly increased! Cher jumped in and immediately began pretending to seek academic guidance to cover up until I was ready.

My heartbeat grew louder and louder with every second, and I was unsure if I was making the right choice! After closing every conversation, they looked at me, but I could not utter a word! Despite ever-so-desperately wanting to spill the beans all over, my anxiety wouldn't let me speak. About half an hour later, we could feel his urge to return back to work. Ayo got super hasty and yelled, "Summer wanted to tell you something!"

All eyes were suddenly on me... CRAP!

Did I finally seize the chance to shake him off my life entirely?

I awkwardly smiled, looking at everybody and mumbled, "Hey, Brother Avi, I meant to tell you something!"

Brother Avi (smiling): "Yeah, sweetie, go ahead!"

He was too generous a man to speak with; I did not feel that I could do it to him! I had respected him every day of my life, and my anger wasn't for him at all; it was for Aaron! He had always been an older and helpful figure to me, it would be unfair to put him through all this!

Summer: "How have you been? It's been a while since we last met, don't you think?"

Brother Avi: "I'm great! Thanks for asking! And I have been busy studying, so I could not see you girls around either."

I could see Cher and Ayo smashing their heads behind him, at my inability to get to the point. They wouldn't realise that I was trying my best to form the right sentences in my head. I was afraid to lose the coordination of my words with my mouth and embarrass myself before him.

Brother Avi: "Are you sure this is what you wanted to say to me?"

My face flushed, but I still couldn't utter a word.

Cher was growing increasingly impatient and jumped to cut me off in the middle. "No, Brother Avi, Summer is just too uncomfortable to say this, but AARON LIKES HER A LOT!"

He looked at me in disbelief. "What? Since when? And how do you know?"

I looked down to the ground, rubbing my feet against each other, I pulled my hands outside my pocket and unconsciously began peeling off the skin from my fingers... He understood it was true, I was too scared to say anything.

I looked up and replied, "Yes, brother Avi, it's true. Your brother likes me…"

Brother Avi: "I'm so sorry, Samara; I really am!"

Summer: "No, that isn't even the hardest part. There's no problem in liking someone. Had it been that, we would have never come to you! It's normal for anyone our age to have feelings for someone, but what he did after was the scary part!"

Brother Avi: "What do you mean? Did he say something to you?"

Summer: "Yes Brother Avi, we are in great trouble and we need your help!"

We spoke to him for over an hour and told him everything down to the most minute detail. We could see his face transition from extreme anger to helplessness and then to total humiliation. Every time he thought things couldn't get any worse, they did!

Brother Avi: "I'm so sorry, Samara; I am sorry you had to go through something like this because of my brother. (after a pause) But you have my word, I won't let him come near you! Just give me some time..."

Summer: "Yes, Brother Avi. We fuelled the whole scene. We could have been more mature, even involving my friend Valen in this. To be able to understand his thought process. It was because of us that he stepped into your life!"

Brother Avi: 'To be honest, my parents hate him! They always felt that he was a rich street brat to be around Aaron. He was also scolded a lot of times for hanging around with him!'

Summer: "I understand, it was our stupid plan! We thought we could play around for a while; it was mindless and pathetically petty on our part. And trust me, if it weren't that serious, we would have never come to you. But I had to ensure my safety and not let his next move scare me all the time!"

Brother Avi: "I understand, kid. I'm happy that you chose to tell me. Although you should've come to me even before; he could be corrected right then."

He said this to us and left assured.

The three of us stood there, silently satisfied. We had nothing left to say anymore. It was all we ever thought of, ever imagined. It was over now, and we did not know how to feel...

The next day...

Aaron climbed down from his bicycle and walked up to me when I arrived at school. Filled with rage, he announced, "I'm sorry; you will never hear from me again..."

He did not even dare to speak to me eye to eye. Looking down at the ground, he expected to hear a reply from me; I said nothing.

He waited for a response, but eventually left.

Valen came to me later that day and said that Aaron met him too. He apologized to him and Jude for his misbehaviour that day. After all this crap, this chapter of *Aaron: The Creep*, was finally over!

2 years later...

'Did we do a little extra?' I would often have these internal conflicts.

'We should have confronted him properly, rather than going straight to his brother and complaining...' the angelic voice insisted.

'Do you think there was any part of him that was willing to listen? Moreover, your reputation was burning down to the ruins; could you afford that?' the devil inside compelled.

'But I ruined his bond with his brother? Don't you get that? What is more important to you? A person's life or your reputation?' the angelic voice questioned.

'Obviously, your reputation—he should have been the one to care about his image before his family, if he ever did! Doing the kind of things he did, what did he think, there wouldn't be any consequences? You would never take any actions?' the devil questioned.

'She has a point! Anyway, what's done is done. We can only continue to live like this. I did ruin someone's life to ensure my security. I sure am a jerk in taking such a step, but he wasn't some naïve kid either! He did mindless things and is now facing their repercussions.

That's it. Brother Avi is super mature. He will carry this on his shoulders all his life!' the angelic voice rationalized.

Yeah, you're right! I have no choice but to acknowledge this and move on with life...

Cher and Ayo had also moved out of the city for their higher studies; my social circle had dangerously slimmed. Brother Avi moved abroad for his job.

Both Valen and I had gotten into a relationship—just not with each other!

We were still friends; at least that's what we told everyone. Back then, after the whole incident closed, I tried confessing my feelings for him. Ironically, that very day, Valen came up to me and told me about his new *girlfriend*. I could not comprehend my feelings as I turned numb.

I was heartbroken; why wouldn't I be? He was my best friend after all! What felt even worse was that he never told me about her until then. There was nothing more precious than our friendship, or maybe that was just me.

His girlfriend was very sweet; what affected me was the time he stopped giving 'us'. He would take her to all our hangout spots, and call her up every time I asked him to meet me. I tried developing a thick skin because he was all I knew here, all I ever wanted to be with!

I felt for all that mattered, it was better this way as he was happy with both of us.

Everything changed after his girlfriend discovered the depths of our friendship. She grew insecure about having me around him, thinking he'd grow fonder. She began meddling in all our hang-ups and conversations! It felt as if she wanted to know whatever we were discussing, and if it wasn't significant, why even talk? I had been feeling lonely, super lonely all the while, and I couldn't even talk with my best friend! This made me suppress my feelings because he never tried to protect our friendship. I couldn't be the only one dragging. We also started fighting with each other more frequently; some of them being brutally uncomfortable. We had consciously built a void between us to be able to reduce these arguments. It often broke my heart to see my best friend pretending to barely know me. We eventually drifted apart, it was better for both of us.

It was during this time that I met Reece…

Reece had extremely polarizing tendencies, he wasn't my rebound. We were never officially in a 'relationship', but there was a part inside the both of us that craved a certain companionship. We had mutually confessed deep passions for each other but could never comprehend if it was truly "love." We had this sort of affair for around six months that I couldn't share with any living soul.

Reece never admitted it, but he kept a close check on all the guys around me. The worst part was that he had sensed my older feelings for Valen. He did not understand what I had for Valen was out of deep passions during a phase of my life. I had taken a good amount of time to move past him. Yes, I wasn't ready for any commitment, but Reece was the hardest to love, and for a long time I felt I could keep him safe, until that one day…

…

Flashback…

I received a verification phone call, spilling some dirty laundry from Cinnamon Estate…

I called Reece immediately.

Summer (crying): "Did she touch you?"

Reece: "Trust me, I feel so guilty it happened, I was feeling like a creep. All I could think of was you, Summer. I wanted to do all those things to you!"

Summer: "That's just bullshit? Do I mean anything to you?"

Reece: "You mean the world to me!"

Summer: "Then how could you do this to me? How will I ever live peacefully knowing you slept with someone else?"

Reece: "You don't understand, I could kill myself right now for being this person! I am a jerk! I should have never done this to you; you don't deserve this, you don't deserve me!"

Summer: "Don't you dare say that! I deserve you, all the secrets you hide from the world! And don't you dare do anything to hurt yourself! I need you, Reece; I can't see you wounded...!"

...

I was desperate, desperate for validation, to be seen and acknowledged by somebody. Reece was that someone for me. I could feel myself rotting every single day, experiencing every high and low of all human emotions. And he had his ways, ways of getting stuff done, victimizing himself in every circumstance, normalizing all his wrong-doings. He would flirt with girls around him; tell me he made love to them and present it in the way that he was always the victim of the situation! I never confronted him either, but I would just lose a piece of myself every time he did that. We fought painfully, all the time.

This verbal abuse finally ended after six months when we cut all ties with each other...

Reece became the second "somebody that I used to know" person after Valen.

Amongst all this mess, Aaron had discovered my little "situation" with Reece. Valen was Reece's old-time frenemy, and I found out about this after spending a good amount of time with Reece. I felt that Valen had anyway drifted apart and had been planning to move out for higher studies. There wasn't really a point in telling him all this. Anyway, my situationship would also be at the edge, so I never bothered getting anything between them either!

Coping up was the toughest time in school since I had no friends left. I was alone. I started reconnecting with my batchmates and would endlessly laugh around them and convince myself not to feel lonely by doing this. Sometimes, it even meant clinging on with different groups of people.

I never understood how I came to this state of being. From making more and more friends every day to losing them by the day...

Aaron also realized by this time that I had no one to protect me. Every time we crossed each other in school, I would ignore him, and turn to whoever was around me.

One day, he approached me and burst out instantly,

'Was I not good enough?'

I had no interest in having a conversation. I resisted the whole thing and replied, "Don't bother Aaron; we're way past this. I don't have time!"

Aaron: (screaming) "Why do you have a problem with me? Why have you never seen me or loved me the way I did?"

Summer: "It isn't even about that anymore! Why don't you understand? I'm in love with someone else! Someone you'd rather stay away from..."

Aaron: "Is it that Valen guy?"

Summer: "No, and you have nothing to do with him! Stay out of my matters and trust me, I'll think of bagging an eye on you."

Aaron: "I should have known you were like them! I was blinded by my love for you!"

Summer: "Like them? What do you mean like 'them'? (smirking) You haven't changed a bit over the years, and deep inside I had been feeling bad for you? You still have no respect for talking to a woman, and you convince yourself that you love them! Go chat with a soul or two, then you'll know how to behave with someone. And please open your eyes; you are obsessed with the idea of me; you don't love me!"

Aaron: "Are you telling me who he is or not?"

Summer: "Bug off, you freak!"

Aaron: 'Well then, I have my ways of finding out!'

Summer (leaving): 'All the luck, honeybee...'

This went on for a long time. I felt as though I was achieving something by making myself look happier before him. I started feeling hollow, pretending to be someone else, but it still gave me the thrill of wanting to do more!

We reached the end of our higher secondary school, with tons of memories, both good and bad ones! With a heart still heavy, I was finally done with my life here in the city, and it was the right time for me to start a new one.

A part of me was desperate to leave the place as early as possible; the other half was scared of the unknown. I had been admitted to one of the premier design colleges. I never expected to see myself take this big a leap from what I had been doing until then. I had no tangible plans for my life. I just wanted to do something different. Secretly hoped it would not be convenient for my parents to compare me with anyone. I had completely convinced myself that hustling the hardest to stand out was the only way to go! Even if it meant standing alone, that was the path I chose.

The happiest part was that I wouldn't have to see Aaron! Never again in my life!

3 months later...

Ayo had come home for her semester break, and after days I was glad to have a familiar face around. I was literally walking into a new chapter of my life and I needed somebody to share it with. It's ironic how we, ever-so-desperately wish to achieve something all our lives and when we actually do, we don't feel anything anymore! Ayo and I would usually meet around 5:30 pm every evening.

One day, I went out to get some groceries. I had informed her of my delay that day, asking if we could catch up around 6 pm, but the work wasn't complete. It didn't bother her much since she was napping in the evening. But for unforeseen circumstances, I reached home terribly late, ready to be scolded by my sweetheart! I came back home at around 7 pm and saw her walking on the streets with Aaron!

Given these guys had been neighbours it wasn't an issue, but she was MY FRIEND; it appeared extremely unlikely!

I wasn't pleased with their little union, so I decided to give her the benefit of doubt and not interrupt her until she was done with her little 'catch-up'!

She called me home after fifteen minutes.

Summer: "What was that, Ayo?"

"Dude, why is this kid so annoying?" she said, yawning.

"Well, shouldn't I be the one to ask what you were doing with that exact annoying kid?" I gasped.

Ayo: "Give me a moment; I really need to process things right now..."

She went to the washroom behind to kill her drowsiness and sat before me.

Summer: "Tell me what happened, will you?"

Ayo: "This kid needs to learn some manners!"

Summer: "Enlighten me, Darling!"

Ayo: "He came to my house and I was sleeping super peacefully, dreaming about you know, money! He first knocked on the door. Now the thing about my house is, that all the sounds echo like crazy, he knocked and my Nanny called up my brother, who he plays with every day. But he told Nanny that he wasn't here to meet him; he wanted to meet me! I am super sure that he would have seen you leave, so he seized the opportunity to speak to me."

Summer: "Just get to the point, sweet bun!"

Ayo: "So he called for me, and my Nanny told him that I was sleeping. He was so mannerless and impatient to meet that he said, 'I really want to meet her, there's something extremely important that I have to discuss with her, etc.' that he almost insisted on getting to my room to talk!"

Summer: "If your whole setup is finished, can we please get to the point?"

Ayo: "Patience Babydoll, patience. Nanny came and hastily woke me up, and I got so pissed! I went outside to meet him, and do you know what he said to me?"

'What?' I asked.

Ayo: "That you are a slut!"

Summer: "WHAT????"

Ayo: "I'm so stupid; I'm so stupid; I can't believe this happened."

Summer: "Ayo, wake up!!! I don't have time for this; tell me what he said!"

Ayo: "I don't really remember how it began, but he said something like, 'You don't know what kind of girl Samara is!"

Flashback to 30 minutes before...

[Aaron and Ayo's conversation]

Aaron: "I have seen girls like her all my life, but I did not think she was one of them. You need to stay away from her or you'll become one just like her!"

Ayo: "What is all this bullshit? Are you really bitching about my best friend to me?"

Aaron: "I have seen her around boys; she is a slut, I can prove it to you!"

Ayo: "Are you crazy? Do you even know the meaning of that word, to be calling her the 's' word!? The very person you once loved?"

Aaron: "I know very well and that's exactly what hurts me the most! I understand what a girl is by how she behaves. You are like a sister to me, and also her friend, but you should see what I saw, and you'll know the whole truth about it."

Ayo: "What 'it'?"

Aaron: "You know 'it'?"

Ayo: "No, please explain to me what 'it' is...?"

Aaron: "You are too naïve to be her friend; consider it something like attention. She craves men's attention, and she keeps dancing around them asking for it. I'm sure that's exactly why her relationship with her boyfriend didn't work out! It's a good thing she is going away from here; I won't have to see the hopeless desperation anymore! Where is she going, by the way?"

Ayo: "To a premier design college!"

Aaron: "Wow, she'll find more attention there! I'm sure there'll be boys like her too! It disgusts me to even think about it."

End of flashback...

Ayo: "I feel so dumb, Summer! He was bullshitting about you in front of me, and I didn't even smack him in the face!"

Summer (laughing): "What? Why would you do that?!"

Ayo: "Why not? This is so stupid; I should have taught this guy a lesson! And what is all this whole narrative about?"

Summer: "Also, why did you tell him about my college!?? He was just trying to trigger you and get this information out! You did that for him! And how does he know that my relationship didn't work out?! I only told him about being with someone and never the fact that it ended."

Ayo: "He is a stalker, Summer. And because you chose not to give in to his love, now he is calling you a whore for attention! This is all really messed up!"

Summer: "You know what, Ayo? I don't want to make the mistake I made two years ago! He wants to see how I react to this and confront him before leaving the city! I'm not going to do that at all... I can't have him beg me at my feet pleading for his love over and over again; it's too exhausting!"

Ayo: "But, honestly, his theory was so funny! He saw you with a bunch of guys and took the effort to pick me up from my place to tell me all this?"

We laughed at the whole scenario and left back home.

Reece and I had broken all our contact with each other. After months of not speaking to each other, I received a text from a new number by Valen's contact asking to meet him before leaving! I was surprised as it would have been close to 11 months since we hadn't been in any significant touch. I wondered if this might be because we would never meet again as old friends.

I agreed to meet at his place the next day.

I reached his place and could sense an unwelcoming energy in the air. As I was entering, I saw another pair of shoes lying there; I wondered if he would have called other people in there too, I thought we were going to meet alone. As I went to Valen's room, I saw him looking at his phone...

I went to pat him on the shoulder when I saw him burning with rage. He showed me his phone with my pictures.

There were various pictures of me with different guys from my class. None of them with clear faces except for mine... The way they all looked was as though I was sharing an intimate association with them!

Summer (shocked): "What is all this!?"

Valen: "Shouldn't I be the one to ask you that?"

Summer: This is all a misunderstanding, Valen. Where did you get this all from? Somebody has played with these!"

Valen: "Then what do you have to say about this!"

Passing me his phone with a picture of Reece and me. The only picture that couldn't have been taken as any misunderstanding. It was a picture we had taken together where he held me very close to his body and both of us were smiling at each other, partially dressed. Someone had hacked my phone and taken those private moments. I felt attacked as these were my memories. But looking at that image in the cluster with others, it all looked as though I were an escort! It suddenly hit me that Valen hated Reece more than anything in the whole world!

"How did you get all this? This is a serious invasion!" I screamed!

Aaron walked out of the washroom, and looking at me, he smirked, "Hi Summer!"

It was him, I was sure... No one would even care to dig as much for this information but him. But, the real question was, why? I had no connection with any of them except for Reece.

Who was I kidding, for how long could I have hidden our secret?

This was his revenge plot! It suddenly hit me, Aaron forged these pictures to turn Valen against me.

Valen: "You could have done anything in the whole wide world, Summer. I never knew you were a girl like this! I thought you were different!!! But you have ended up being even worse."

Summer (defending): "Why are you even listening to him? This is all a misunderstanding and he is the root of it all! Can't you see all this? Why don't you trust me?"

Valen (still in remorse): "And let myself be hurt again? Sure!"

Summer: "Please don't talk to me like that! What have I done to deserve all this? We can talk this all out, trust me!"

Valen (anger turning to disappointment): "I did, Summer. I did... trust you more than anyone in the world, beyond what anyone said!"

Summer: "No Valen, this isn't how it works!

(smirking sarcastically) This is really the moment when you should have given no fu*ks about what people are saying! Did you even try to understand where I am coming from?"

Valen: "I can't do this, all your lies and manipulation. You can just not keep fooling me like always! I understand now; you make this face and pretend like nothing's happened..."

Summer: "I am not good with confrontations. It aches my chest and I palpitate!"

Valen: "How bloody inconvenient, isn't it? Running away from the truth like it's so bothersome for Madame Samara."

Summer (tearing up, still grinning): 'How was it ever trust, Valen? When you were supposed to trust me, you fumbled. For you, great friendship is only for as long as you are having a great time, right? For when you need an escape and it's the happiest thing in the world?

One hardship, just one hardship and you stumbled it all up!"

Valen: "You talk to me about trust? Then, why didn't you tell me about Reece?"

Summer: "We don't have to do this, Valen. Don't bring Reece into this mess; this isn't really the right time to talk about him. I will tell you everything about him, I am not ready right now."

Valen: "Again, how bloody convenient? And this 'Pillar of High Esteem' was speaking of 'trust' and 'fumbling in friendships'? (tearing up) Trust me Summer, of all the spineless people I've come across in my life, you are the one most hollow! You have no foundation; forget about having a spine!"

[There was silence... A painful bit of silence]

Summer (gasping): "I don't have anything to say. But trust me, you are going to regret saying this all your damn life."

Valen (breaking down): "Tell me honestly, did you ever get so close to him (looking towards Aaron)?"

Summer: "I never did!"

Valen: "Remember, we all laughed when we read those letters, but then what was all that?"

Aaron (evil smiling): "She is exactly what you're thinking right now, Valen. We all should have known it all along! YOU HAVEN'T SEEN WHAT I SAW! I have evidence to show the many guys has slept with! She even loved you, Valen! And knowing all this pretty well, she made you the pawn to throw me off from her life!"

Summer: "BE IN YOUR LIMITS, AARON!"

Valen was thunderstruck. His face froze. His world was at a standstill. I was shattered; Aaron had been tracking me for I don't know how long. He knew everything about me: first Reece, then my buried-down love for Valen!

Valen: "Answer me, Summer; is it true?"

Summer (cracking): "I'm really sorry; I have to leave."

(I could feel myself breaking by every passing second)

Valen (screaming): "Stay right where you are and tell me, is it true, Summer?"

After all this time, whatever I did for Valen went down in vain. He did not even respect our friendship enough to have this intervention with me alone. Aaron was enjoying every bit of this and Valen was giving him more reasons to...

Summer: "YES! It's true, it was always true. I have loved you since the time we became friends. I'd hate myself every day for failing to confess my feelings for you because I kept my friendship above any other. I never wanted to lose you. And why didn't I ever tell you before? Because I ain't your type. We were never meant to be! I did not want your rejection or your pity, Valen. It hurts hiding things from you, but it would hurt me even more knowing that you wouldn't understand even if I told you! I was always affected by your relationship with your "perfect" girlfriend; I was also happy that at least then I would be able to not think about you anymore! And to be honest, I don't think I feel for you the way I did before and it's good that I had been given the time to grow apart and move on."

Valen was still there, struck by these revelations.

Summer: "I met Reece when I was trapped in my own mess; I was not ready for anything with him, or at least that's what I thought! I was in a verbally abusive relationship with restrictions on talking about it with anyone. I am still not in the right mental state to talk about this but that hardly makes any difference in your life since it isn't 'convenient', right? It was much later that I got to know that you both hated each other so much! And since I hadn't been in contact with the two of you, I never thought of calling you up to 'clear' the air."

The was a painful breeze of silence…

Summer (gasping): "But you know what hurts me the most? You believed it when Aaron called me a 'whore'! You did not break his nose like the first time, when you trusted me. Forget even taking the courage to ask me the real truth! And what evidence does he have? These pictures that have been taken layering double exposure and reverse angle? It's easier for a 10th-grader now to mask reality on Photoshop. I am telling you the only one real here is with Reece, and these moments were very private and special. I mean, at least they were for me. And it isn't cool to circulate someone's emotions? I am pretty sure that the whole school might be thinking of me as a whore now, but if I can't convince an old friend, I am sure I cannot convince the world either. I'll probably have to live with this tag! And again, why? Because I rejected him two years back?! Have a great life ahead, Valen. You have no idea what I have suffered, but I don't think I can anymore. It's better for both of us that we never see each other again…"

I ran away from his house, crying…

I knew I couldn't escape my fate being here; I had only two weeks left before leaving the city. I isolated myself from everyone, except Ayo. The school being closed was the only benefit for me then.

-end of chapter-

Chapter 3:
Runaway Disguises

Six months later...

Present day...

New City, New Place, New People. Leaving behind all the mess with Reece, Valen and Aaron.

I am Samara Laine 2.0.

Ambitious, happy and probably better now... I cut those ties with my past self entirely.

Within six months, I could feel this transformation in me. I had created a bubble around myself, and hardly anybody could ever even get close to me. For the rest of the world (here), I was an arrogant woman with a high narcissistic quotient and lofty esteem. I did not want any recollection of who I had been before. I changed my number, and social handles. I cut my contacts with people who could remind me of anything remotely related to my past. Aaron had never connected with me on any social platform, so that wasn't much of a bother.

I could not give my head that hard time again; I wanted to remain anonymous and underground. People at college could only know the things about me I approved of. Making an impression as straight-headed and unempathetic. But all these led to one thing ultimately, I had nobody here to talk wholeheartedly to, like Ayo and Cher.

Growing up was a shitload of experience, and it only got worse as I moved out of my comfort space. I developed severe attachment issues after having lost people I once termed as my "constants"! This has greatly shaped my equation with the friends I make now. It's a skilful and conscious shift from a free spirit to a cold, calculative person. Both, the needs of their respective ages! For how long could you be irresponsibly ignorant? I have become more vulnerable and self-guarding. A daily share of cultural shocks reminds me of what used to be but ain't anymore!

It seems like everyone is living similar lives. We grind all day working on assignments, and then show the best versions of our lives on the 'gram, ignore our feelings and then sob ourselves to sleep! Delusional or not, it somehow pans out our character arc from what we were to what we are striving to become. It pushes us to become like a new person!

A few days after thinking and living life like this, a longtime junior from school, Nico called me up to ramble about his "teen" problems. While speaking to him, I inquired about people around (and also, Aaron) since he was his classmate.

Nico (astonished): "Dude, you have no idea, he has changed completely!"

Samara (confused): "What do you mean changed? Like how?"

Nico: "He has become a weird-saintly sort of man now! He even comes to class wearing beaded bracelets and a huge *teeka* on his forehead straight out of the temple at 7 am, every day.

Samara: "I mean, how is that a bad thing?"

Nico: "Wait for it, Samara. You're not listening."

Samara: "Ok, Ok! I'm sorry, carry on!"

Nico: "He says he has trained his body to refrain from meek attachments or meaningless desires! It's insane, I don't even know how to explain this to you! He tells people that he has memorized the sacred text, which is great by the way, but who asked? Nobody cares about him. One day, in the Chemistry lab, he rambled something so loudly that caught the classes' attention. He linked the changing colour of mixing two chemicals to the spiritual disorder of human's subconscious mind and their intentions. Like, I don't know how rational am I sounding right now but that's the point, it's totally stupid! He tries to outsmart everyone; from subject teachers to the cleaning staff. Trust me, no one even bothers about him, but I guess that's how he amplifies and makes everyone notice him! Feels like he craves attention. It's hilariously embarrassing. He also says he wants to master being away from all "worldly pleasures".

Samara (laughing): "Whoa! That's something! Well, if he says that he doesn't care about worldly pleasures, there shouldn't be a soul happier than me!"

Nico: "I don't know, Samara. He isn't like the rest of us, he has this aura around him, as if he joined a cult of some spiritual sort. I have come across many people in my life, but no one is like him!"

Samara: "What else does he do in class?"

Nico: "He picks fights with everyone to put down everyone! No girl wants to be around him because he treats them disrespectfully. For any group project, no one wants to take him because then they'll have to *be around him*! He isn't even great at studies to carry this kind of arrogance!"

Samara: "He wasn't worthy of being friends since the start, I suppose. And as you said, I can safely assume that he must have become a part of some hippie cult. He blames his false doings as some part of a "grand scheme". The only problem for you guys is that you go to the same class as him. He's after all a kid crying for attention and will do anything to get it! Don't give him the satisfaction of affecting your mind and he'll stop. I learnt it the hard way! As long as he isn't the person I knew years back, we're good."

Nico: "You're right. I wanted to give you the update; I have my matters to deal with, so you had better help me with those first and leave this guy behind!"

We spoke for about an hour, but I felt happy speaking to him since I hadn't heard from him all this time. He wasn't a very integral part of my previous life, or was even slightly involved or aware of the drama, so breaking contact with him wasn't on my agenda.

'But a monk, huh? Whatever makes him stay away from my life then!' I said to myself and got back to sleep, relieved.

...

Three months later...

It had been over nine months of hearing anything from him.

One day around 12:30 am, I finished my assignment and was prepping my bed, I got this notification on my 'gram with his request. It was amusing, he had found my account name, but who cares? My account's private anyway. I don't have to see his face, I needn't be so worried. I ignored it and crashed off to sleep.

A few days later, I got this notification with the same account again. I made sure to block him this time.

...

2 weeks later...

We had to take a survey for one of our group assignments, so our team of five people ran the campaigns of our socials. I had to make my profile public to get as many responses. Within a few hours at night when I was asleep, my 'gram was filled with notifications. Since I had made my account public, the pending requests auto-approved. It hit me that there were two separate accounts from which I had received the request. One that I had ignored first, and the other that I blocked. They both were so identical, that it almost slipped my head. It was him...

He had liked all my posts and below one of my pictures, he commented:

@WeirdAaronusername01: 'Mamma, please be my friend. Love you, Summer, always and forever.'

"WHAT THE F*CK IS THIS GUY DOING???!!!!!"

I completely freaked out.

It had been over five hours since that comment. I immediately blocked him and deleted the comment, hoping not many people would have seen it! I could weirdly sense my past coming my way again. It had taken a great deal to come to where I am today, both mentally and emotionally. I couldn't afford to lose all of it because of this one asshole of a person! What worried me more was that I had never grown past it; rather I had just stopped thinking about it. There was a difference, and this very difference filled my mind with anxiety.

A few days later...

I am in my class till 5:30 p.m. After class, I head towards the campus gate to leave and suddenly spot someone from afar.

'Could that be Aaron?' I thought to myself. Or am I just being delusional now? How and why will he come here? Was it the flash of my eye that made someone else look like him to me?

Anyway, Ayo told him just about my college's name, not the campus location. There were over fifteen campuses across the country. It could be any one. I need to be sure if it is him otherwise, just the trash in my head. In an attempt to confirm if it's him, I head to the other side of the gate to spot him.

'It won't be him,' I tell myself. Somewhere down, I did not want to confirm this.

We had a project discussion today; no hurries to leave for the hostel, which is on the other side of the main campus. I move to the common area for our discussion and try my best to forget about it entirely.

A little later, a girl from one of my courses walked up to me with her friends and said, "Hey Samara, somebody is looking for you at the main gate. He has your picture. He looks a little helpless. I told him about you. But since we did not know him, we couldn't let the guards have him come in. Go meet him!"

FU*KKKKK!

It's him...

I could feel an instant choke in my throat as my feet ran cold and my neck started sweating. How did he come till here!?? Was it because of that comment? I remember not updating my location literally anywhere. Did he find out about all this through the tagged pictures of my friends here? I don't have time to think about all this. I need to figure a way out of this. It's good the guards wouldn't let him in at this hour without verification.

We wind up our group discussions, and it's 9 p.m. My roommate was also here, waiting to leave with me. He must have gone by now, and we should also leave.

I took the same girl to the campus exit and asked her to check if he was still there. There were no absolute exits from the campus; all link up to this one here. I don't want to face him. There's got to be some other way. I looked around and saw the Costume Design Team prepping for their upcoming event.

My friend, Yana is in the Team. I call her up to explain the whole situation.

"Come inside the green room backstage; I'm here. We were doing our makeup trials; we could do it on you!" Yana reassured.

"Darling, that's a great idea; I'm coming," I was overjoyed!

The theme of their show was 'Broadway Drag'; I couldn't be any happier. They transformed my face into something completely unrecognizable.

I gave a basic brief to the MUA: 'the bizarre, the better'. After over an hour, it had been 10 p.m., and these guys had done an amazing job. I looked like the female version of RuPaul (just brown and without the inflated hairdo and lashes). Our college gates closed at 10:30 p.m., and the guards had started sending us off. We had booked our cab from the green room itself, I could not afford to walk the way out.

After ten minutes, the cab was there. We run towards the cab without glancing elsewhere for a second. I got in, and I spotted him looking at everyone.

Someone from the crowd outside recognised me and screamed my name waving. Aaron heard him and ran towards our cab hastily.

"Can you please drive fast? We are in a bit of trouble here," I begged the driver, running breathless.

He sped the car through the university's narrow lanes. Just then, Aaron jumped in front of us. My heart was trembling with fear; why was he doing all this? The car had slowed due to the rush of the hour. Aaron walked up to my window as I pretended to use my phone and gave a loud blow. I looked at him because of the jumpscare, but he failed to recognize me due to my heavily disguised facade...

The deception had worked!

He moved past us as the driver yelled at him for his civic misbehaviour. We left from there, and after having covered some distance, I turned back to have a look. He also turned around abruptly, and we made eye contact.

"SHITTTT!" I screamed.

He saw me and started running towards us... My heart rate shot up as I yelled at the driver to speed up, and I jumped from my bed, all drenched in sweat...

.

.

.

It was just a dream...

I got up and looked at the clock; it was 3:47 a.m.

I was watching a murder mystery when I crashed off to sleep and hadn't turned it off. I took out the earpieces and shut my laptop down.

Although it was just a dream, it felt just so real, I really hope this never happens.

...

3 months later...

I received a new message request on the gram.

Is it him? I recalled blocking him last time. My account was still in public mode, it is because of that? Upon checking other notifications, I found the same username commenting on a lot of my posts.

@WeirdAaronusername_02 commented, *'You look so beautiful, Summer; tell me at once whether you have a boyfriend or not. Answer me!'*

I freaked out for a moment and made sure to immediately delete all the comments he made on the posts. I opened my DM and found his message request.

@WeirdAaronusername_02: "Who is Khalil? Brother, friend or boyfriend?"

(Khalil was really just a batchmate I spoke to since we were in the same class. Someone with a public profile might have tagged us both in a picture from the college events.)

Samara: "You have nothing to do with it."

@WeirdAaronusername_02: "Don't play these games, and answer me."

Samara: "I am not obligated to tell you anything about my life. Bugger off, freak!"

I blocked him immediately. Khalil was a nobody to me. But I certainly knew that the conversation wouldn't have ended there. He had no direct access to my life other than these petty attempts to look at other people's profiles. Wasn't he done ruining my reputation in school that he was attempting for my college folks now? Experiences from the last time had taught me that, the more you tell him, the deeper he wants to dig. Better let him be in the dark about whatever I am.

1 month later...

Kai, my childhood friend and old-time's heartthrob, messaged me. He was now a great gossip partner who had moved close to my house back in the city. I hadn't heard from him in a long while.

Kai (attaching a screenshot): Hey! Could you ever in your life believe that Yoshi could get into a rave party?

(It was a picture with a bunch of girls surrounded by neon lights at some party)

Samara: How are you? It's been one heck of a while, man! I'm sure those guys must mean "fun" in that context!

Kai: Yeah, that's true, but Yoshi and stuff? I never thought I would be capable of even thinking of something like that!

Samara (chuckling): You're right. But Yoshi is one of my best friends. Let me just ask her and I'm sure you'll know what you want.

Kai: You don't get it; this could potentially be the most mind-blowing flip story of my life, if that ever happened! Remember how she used to be so naïve?'

Samara: Never mind you; I'm sure the world has made more people and flip stories for you! I just wanna see your expectations break!

Kai: Ask her ASAP and tell me!

Samara: For laughing out loud, what makes you so curious?

Kai: Nothing, I want to have my mind blown away! It's kind of my guilty pleasure now. Also, I could trade a secret for another if you want!

Samara: What secret?

Kai: Tell me first!

Samara: I will, I will! Don't worry! But you tell me first!

Kai: Who is this fan of yours?

Samara: No! Why? How do you know about him now?

Kai: He texted me out of the blue.

Samara: Why you? And how do you know him?

Kai: That's what I asked myself, why me? Doesn't he live close to our houses?

Samara: He literally lives right in front of my house! Picture this: our gates open exactly opposite each other!

Kai: A stalker or a fan? Can I get the entire gossip?

Samara: You wouldn't wanna know, goes back 5 years! He's a freak who's made my life a living hell! I mean, not really, you get what I mean; I don't want to talk about it.

Kai: Damn, you have a five-year-long fan following! You never told me!

Samara: Seriously, Kai? It's nothing to be proud of, or to even be sharing with you guys! Also, he is really just a freak, so no real brownie points there.

Kai: Anyway, he was asking me to send screenshots of your posts.

Samara: WHAT? What did he say?

Kai: He said he loved you and some crap, then asked me to send screenshots, which I didn't, obviously!

Samara: Thank you so much, love!

Kai: And.......

Samara: And?

Kai: He also mentioned something about someone named "Reece."

Samara: Wait, what?

Kai: Is this the Reece that I'm thinking about?

Samara: I know Kai, but don't, please don't!

Kai (teasing): Seriously, Samara, Reece? Of all people, Reece!

Samara: Trust me, even I wanna know that. Why Reece, of all living men in the world!

Kai: Sure, no pressure! He asked, 'Who has Summer been dating since Reece?' And I was like... Wait what?

Samara: Just block him love, will you!? Also, can you send me a screenshot of his texts? I am trying to collect his stalky-ass messages!

Kai: I would, but since I denied sharing your posts with him, he unsent all his texts!

Samara: Damn it! By the way, Yoshi texted; they were just having fun and weren't at any rave smokin' stuff!

My situation with Reece had been an extremely private affair, but now I felt my past was coming back to me. I had been living each day of my life trying to run away from it, but even after all this time, it hadn't spared my life!

The next week, I received another message request from a new account which, to my horror, was Aaron's.

@WeirdAaronusername_03: 'Hello Summer, this is Aaron. I lost my previous account due to password-related issues, so this is my new one. Please follow this one. Please don't get mad at me. When you come home, I will definitely talk to you. P.S.: I love you, Summer.'

? ? ?

What part of the interaction did he not understand exactly? Password-related issue? I had blocked him; how hard was this to comprehend? I was enraged by all this! What exactly does he think of himself?! How is he talking to me like nothing wrong ever happened? I literally felt like throwing my phone away. This time I wanted to make sure not to leave any room for self-generated comprehension.

Samara: I don't understand how to explain to you that I'm done with this crap! For f*ck's sake, stop this! It's been over five years now, please end this bullcrap! I have explained this to you enough number of times, but I can't anymore! You have been acting like a major creep since I don't remember how long! I don't like you, never did, nor ever will! You turn my friends against me, convince them I am characterless and then expect me to exchange pleasantries with you? Like we are some long-lost friends? Either you are mad, or willing to turn me into one. Whichever it is, just keep your shit together and stop bothering me! I swear to God, you'll never hear from me again. I must ignore you for the rest of my life!

I was determined to never talk to him ever again from that very moment. But for the record, I made sure to take every screenshot as evidence for filing a cyber harassment case. I also had to ensure, with absolute certainty, that I wasn't repeating a mistake I had made years ago. My actions were confused as advances. I should have understood all his reinvention into 'a monk' was a mere freak show! He is still the same old creep living in his delusions, expecting me to take part in it too! After all this time, he hadn't changed at all!

-end of chapter-

Chapter 4:
F*d Up World

15 March 2020

Radio buzzing;

"The first cases of COVID-19 were reported on 30 January 2020 in three towns of the country, among three medical students who had returned from Wuhan, the epicentre of the pandemic. Lockdowns are announced for the country from 25 March 2020, and all modes of transportation will be closed until any further communication."

It's a Sunday and I am in the lab working with my batchmates. Our first reaction to this news was sheer joy and relief since we had overloading project submissions the next week. It took us more than a moment to analyse that everyone around us was hurrying to leave the campus to go back home. There is utter chaos, with everyone packing up to leave with whatever modes of transport are available. We got this tip that the flights would not be functional after a week; the airline prices skyrocketed and the trains were overbooked.

The world had shut its doors in our faces and there was commotion and panic all around. We were constantly receiving calls from our parents. A few distant family members were diagnosed as positive. High security was forced in all the public places. Cafés, cinema houses, even our college amphitheatre, all of them were sealed by the officials, leaving only certain grocery shops, which were again heavily monitored, with shielding masks high up. Everyone looked like a modern masked warrior.

With only a little sum in my bank, I cannot book a flight back home. There aren't many train options either so I decided to pool in with a friend and took the longer route back home.

Starting from the western edge, all the way up north, and then to my home around the centre. After comprehensive assessments and booking delays, we left the campus early on 16th March.

Extremely paranoid, and taking the best measures of barely having any physical contact with the surroundings, we board our train. My compulsive obsession emerged with constant sanitization and the urge to sterilize our luggage every hour. After travelling across the country with a transit of around 7 hours, I reached home early in the morning on 18th March. Counting each penny in my pocket since I had no more than Rs. 200 in my account and bare cash to pay to the rickshaw guy. The journey had been rather overwhelming. I was welcomed home by my mom. We prayed to God for our health and safety.

As I was rushing inside, I saw Aaron standing...

I ignored him completely and after long hours of a deep cleansing shower, took a good nap. I updated all my friends that I was back in town. Just then I also saw a floating message on the notifications bar.

@WeirdAaronusername_04: 'Hey, welcome home!'

I took a screenshot of the message, blocked the account, and went outside to meet my friends, *socially distanced*. Cher and Ayo hadn't come back yet. I had planned to tell them about everything this creep had done over the past year and a half while I was in college. After confirming with my mother, I gathered that Brother Avi had not been home yet, he was put up in his place abroad with his wife-to-be. Our little busting session with Brother Avi had been a five-year-old affair, and I did not wish to indulge him anymore. He had helped us then, and we were extremely grateful to him.

The next day, I woke up to another different notification;

@WeirdAaronusername_05: 'My favourite colour is, FYI blue, Summer!'

I recalled a friend (with a public account) tagging me in a post from one of our excursions. It had a picture with our batchmate in the frame with the caption, 'FYI, blue is @Summer's favourite colour.'

He was stalking all my friends, and also wanted me to notice that he knew stuff about me.

I ignored it, took a screenshot and opened his account to block it, where the bio said 'Too lazy, that's all. That is no reason to worry, okay?'

He had been turning creepier by the day. I could not think of anything else, but to piss him off by not giving him the attention he needed.

Within a span of 2 months, I'd receive a message from a new account almost twice every week. I had grown extremely scared.

...

@WeirdAaronusername_06: 'Summer Mama, hey!'

@WeirdAaronusername_07: 'Summer, in front of our homes, there are two cute puppies. Have you seen them? (Yes/No?)'

@WeirdAaronusername_08: 'Summer, I have tried to change my username so that any confusion between other people and my name can be avoided. Please be my friend, Mamma.'

@WeirdAaronusername_09: 'Summer, you can keep my password too, but please, Mamma, be my friend; I am feeling sad.'

@WeirdAaronusername_10: (Bio: Homesick, ill, fever, stomach upset, not Covid, can't come, that's why.)

He sent me a picture in a one-view mode of a pink rose, he was literally home, why would he even write that!?

@WeirdAaronusername_11: (Bio: Almost recovered) 'I'm too tired, Summer.'

@WeirdAaronusername_12: 'I want to see your 56th, 57th, 58th, 59th, and 60th posts, please. And be my Instagram friend.'

[Back in college, I had put up this story with the caption, '*I love all the things that don't make sense like I love you*' (a song lyric reference of 'Nobody Knows' by Mansionz - the Blackbear and Mike Posner duo).]

@WeirdAaronusername_13: 'I love all the sensible things, like I love you, Bearess.'

Also, why the hell was he referring to me as 'Mamma'? I literally had no idea what kind of content did he consume.

This guy had been going crazy!! After a 2-weeks break, when I felt that he might have been tired of this, he did the most bizarre thing in this world. Ayo had come back home during this while and she sent me a screenshot of his message.

@WeirdAaronusername_14: "Hello Ayo, this is Aaron. Please let Summer know about my account and see my posts; you can also see them. It will be for everyone. This is my first step in spreading the Almighty Lord's consciousness, and I want Summer to see my posts without fail. Thank you."

Cher received a similar sort of request and message from him. After setting up the ground, he sent me a long text two days later along the same line, and even without reading the text entirely, I blocked the account.

@WeirdAaronusername_14: 'Hello Summer, this is Aaron. Please follow me, it's my request. The sole reason for my long absence was that I thought you made your account private so that I wouldn't get distracted seeing your posts; I know you were unhappy. I understood something entirely different now. Time to remove phase differences between us, please. Seeing my posts will bring you immense happiness and peace. Also, I saw all your stories and posts till 14th Feb, the day you made your account private, I was there. I was Always there for you. But I could not make an account then, since time wasn't in my favour.'

This had become maddening... He was just not stopping. I couldn't comprehend anything anymore. I started losing my sleep merely thinking about all this. He had to be stopped! Brother Avi was also not here, he could have helped us in this whole scenario. Although, for the record, he was younger than me, his actions were making me feel more and more unsafe about myself and my mental being. It was as if I had been living a life of fear, cautious of his every move.

One day, Ayo and I were discussing the whole situation, and Ayo's mom suddenly entered the room. We were discussing whether we should involve his mother in this scenario. Ayo's mom overheard us and was curious to know what we girls had been up to.

Ayo: "It's nothing, Mom. This guy Aaron has been troubling Summer for a long time now."

Ayo's Mom: "Who Aaron? Dr. Yahya's son, Aaron? Our neighbour Aaron?"

Ayo: "Yes Mom. There's no need to overreact."

Ayo's Mom: "You girls seriously need to take a break, you put your heads a little too much in overthinking."

I preferred to say nothing in the whole conversation. I somehow knew there wouldn't be a point really.

Ayo: "What do you mean, Mom?"

Ayo's Mom: "I just mean that you guys must have misunderstood things. That kid is too pious to trouble anyone. He has become almost saintly these days."

Ayo: "Of course, you have fallen prey to his false narrative as well."

Ayo's Mom: "And what's really false about it? Enlighten me, my child?"

Ayo (growing hesitant): "He is a total freak and none of you can see it. We know who he really is and what all he has done to Summer all this while."

I was now getting extremely uncomfortable by the whole interaction, so I decided to leave from there to get some fresh air in their garden.

I couldn't help myself but feel so small, so trivial. It was as if someone had grabbed my throat from the inside and was threatening to slice it. He never screamed at me, I couldn't complain anyone that! Never abused me, just created a menace that was more of a personal conflict, than a civil or domestic issue.

But why was I even having this dialogue with myself? All I could ever feel was a constant unrest, a constant fear that someone was watching over me... When I slept, when I wept, when I bathed, someone was always there...

I was a prey out in the jungle and the predator was on his knees all the time to hunt me down. From my phone, inside my house, in my room; like what the f*ck was this state of living even?

Ayo came out after some time...

"We are doomed, Summer!" she exclaimed.

Samara: "What is it? What happened inside?"

Ayo: "We are seriously doomed, Summer. It took me a thirty-minute-long fight with *my* mother to explain that he had been chasing you. Till the end, she wasn't convinced about this. How are we ever going to convince his mom about it?"

Samara: "I have no idea. I don't know what to do at all. I have been stuck in my head and feeling miserable for so long now. I am afraid of using the 'gram, I am afraid that he might come in my house, I don't want to live my life like this. Just tell me what to do!?"

Ayo: "Don't just give up yet, Doll. Let's try and then think of giving up?"

As we were talking, Cher came to join us in.

Cher (looking at me, then questioning Ayo): "Explain the face, Ayo"

Ayo: "We were just thinking of speaking to Aaron's mom, rather than Brother Avi this time. But just then my mom came, and I had a whole argument with her trying to expose his true colours. And it was just my mom, who wasn't willing to believe what had been said. Imagine being able to do this to his mom."

Cher: "Well, we need to assess the situation first. Let's strike up a conversation with Aunt Noreen to analyse her thought process. We need to understand her appetite first and then think of telling her anything."

That's a great way forward. The next evening, we were at Ayo's place talking about life and college in general. We strategically placed ourselves to get a glimpse of Aunt Noreen.

She came out and smiled at us,

Aunt Noreen: "What are you girls up to, out in the open? Aren't you scared of the pandemic?"

Cher: "We have taken all our precautions, Aunt."

Ayo (diverting): "All this has been so scary lately. Summer and I had just been talking about how people have been coping with everything. But this quarantine thing is so hard with people who have never actually spent their time together in one home. We hear these cases of domestic conflicts going around."

Aunt Noreen: "That's just life, some people cope with it, rest crib about it!"

Samara: "It isn't just like that, Aunt! This isn't as black and white, not everyone is bold enough to stand up and voice themselves, a lot of factors are usually involved."

Aunt Noreen: "It's true, factors are involved but what's the point of a life where you are making no effort to be happy and falling prey to the circumstances."

[Things clearly weren't exactly going as we had planned...]

Samara: "Now for example, there's a friend of mine who was in college, her father lost his job before the pandemic and she couldn't rush home like the rest of us due to a lack of money and insanely inflated prices. Her boyfriend, who lived nearby, stayed in the city to be with her through this hard time. Everything had been great between them, but since they actually started living together, they encountered some real issues, involving harsh verbal abuse. At this moment, they have called things off, and still lived in the same house. But once the quarantine is over, they'll walk their own ways..."

Aunt Noreen (laughing and heavily judging): "That's just the worst example you could have given, Samara. Firstly, why does your generation have everything up so casual? Reading between the lines, I am so sure the girl would have pressured the guy to stay home. I cannot even imagine the things she might have done to him. And what is this concept of yours, living in the same house as if there is no social construct? Regulations in a society were made for a reason. Girls these days lack morality, they *just want to screw around with* people like it's nothing. You kids feel that it's the coolest thing to break rules. I am so glad that my Aaron is away from all these messes."

Cher (offended, her pitch was alarming): "What do you mean?"

Aunt Noreen (boasting): "He isn't interested in all this crap! He is a monk-in-the-making and wouldn't be swayed by any women's spell."

Samara: "Isn't Brother Avi also staying with his fiancé?"

Aunt Noreen (enraged): "Mind your tongue, he isn't staying with her. They both are just based in the same city. She cooks food at her house and gets it to Avi's house and they accompany each other for just the meals and catch-ups. We have found him a well-cultured girl, *girls unlike yourself,* who like playing with boys on their fingers."

Samara (feeling attacked, but speaking sarcastically): "Aren't you sounding a bit too personal here?"

Cher: "You think too highly of Aaron, maybe he might not be telling you everything..."

Aunt Noreen: "We have raised him too well. There's nothing he doesn't tell us."

Samara: "What if there might be something about him that we know and you don't!"

Aunt Noreen: "And what exactly is that? May I know?"

Just as we were about to speak, Aaron walked in. There wasn't a way he was not listening to this conversation and chose to step in just then.

Aaron (smiling and greeting): "Hi Sister Ayo, Sister Cher."

Aunt Noreen: "See, he greatly respects every female as his sister!"

I felt too attacked by the whole situation and left the place. I tried reaching the corner of the street and sat on the swing, scrolling through my phone.

It's almost 7 p.m. and the sun's down. I kept my phone aside and closed my eyes, thinking of what else could be done with this guy.

I felt a swift wave passing through the bushes, and suddenly my neck was grabbed from behind.

Aaron: "What do you think you were trying to do back there?"

I was choking, unable to speak. I couldn't breathe and my hands and legs were trembling due to the isolation of my blood circulation. I was flapping my feet all over.

Aaron: "Consider this my last warning, I see you around my mom, and I'll expose those pictures to your parents. The ones that took your beloved Valen away. I'll let your parents also know the real you."

He said this and jerked me mid-air, where I couldn't even take a glimpse of him. The grab of his hand was so strong that it left a mark on my neck. I fell down on the ground shaking with fear.

My life is doomed...

-end of chapter-

Chapter 5:
The Plot

The Next day...

I explained last night's episode to Cher and Ayo and how he threatened me with those morphed pictures. I couldn't explain Valen about them; my parents were an even greater gamble.

Cher: "What if we tell the police? Or file against cybercrime? We have evidence of the screenshots!"

Samara: "No chance, my mom will know about all this!"

Ayo (irritated): "She obviously will, Summer. But don't you see, we have no choice here! Certainly, complaining that to his mom isn't going to work. She is too firm!"

Cher: "Ayo's right. Her 'my innocent son' belief is too strong to break. Even if we show the screenshots, she'll say they're edited. Or, she'll say, 'Summer must have swayed him'!"

Samara: "I am sure if Aaron brings up his previous theory, she'll be the first to buy it and put all the blame on me!"

Ayo: "All that aside, Summer. You have to understand this one thing: if we really want to get out of all this, your parents will know. It is the undeniable truth! Otherwise, you can always be where you are, conscious and afraid of his every other move."

Cher: "And he has those morphed pictures of yours. He might send them to your parents to establish his power over you."

Samara: "I don't understand! I feel so stuck, so helpless. That person has single-handedly taken my life down for the past five years. I leave a city, no point; I change my number, he finds it out; I am on any social media, he sniffs me and the people around. I have never felt so helpless in my life! I haven't slept for days. Every time I fall asleep, I have the fear he'll be there tomorrow!"

Cher: "Don't break already. You can't lose this battle. One of my friends here knows a therapist. Let's consult him! Our reflexes have frozen; we might get something new from him."

Ayo: "That's a great idea."

Samara: "I don't think I can!"

Ayo: "We don't know about you, but we can't see you like this anymore. Try out; in the worst-case scenario, we fail. But aren't we failing already?"

.

[I take a day's time to process everything and meet the girls again the next day. It had taken a complete toll on me and I cannot live like this anymore]

Samara: "Ayo, you were right, I should visit a therapist; I don't t*hink I can live my life in misery anymore. All I ever think about is his next action, harming me or my parents!"

...

Fearing the unknown, I sought guidance from many online sources about the guy Cher referred, upon reaching out, I connected with this seasoned, yet retired LMHC professional.

His name is Karin Sharmon.

He lived 20 km away from our house, but that was the best I could do without having Aaron follow me. I had calculated the time when Aaron left to play football. Exactly then, Cher would pick me up from my house and we would go meet him! She would guard me and also carry me through it all. She deserved all the brownie points of my life! I made sure to treat her each day for helping me get through it. We covered our faces entirely with a scarf to not be instantly recognised by anyone. It was Cher's vehicle so the chances of Aaron following me also slimmed. It was probably my biggest risk. Seeking help was the only way out. But, with its unpopularity, I couldn't tell my parents.

I was sceptical about disclosing all the info, so I kept my initial sessions low. We reached his house, which had an attached clinic. Cher left me mid-way and pushed me inside the room. He was right there, examining some files. I was growing super anxious by the second. He smiled at me and offered the seat as I glanced around the interior of the office. It looked like a retirement home with an old Brooklyn vibe. The bricked-walls were filled with his pictures and awards. There were two couches opposite each other where I proceeded to sit. My heart began racing as a drop of sweat fell off my face. I smiled back to greet Dr. Karin and sat on the couch opposite him, my feet wouldn't stop shaking.

Mr. Karin: "Samara Laine, am I pronouncing your name correctly?"

Samara: "Yes, Doctor Karin."

Mr. Karin: "Oh, little lad, don't call me a doctor. If you call me that people will think you're sick and suffering from some disease! Just call me Karin; I'll be as good a help to you only if you talk to me as your confidante, not some boomer. We are good old friends who share life problems. The only difference is, I take a bit of your money at the end!" He said laughing cheerfully.

Samara (chuckling): "Yes, Mr. Karin. Thanks, I was really scared about all this."

Mr. Karin: "Let's work with Karin. Tell me, do your parents know about this little visit of yours?"

Samara: "No, Dr... I mean, Mr. Karin. And they must not, either. What I have come for must not be known by them; otherwise, I will be in great trouble."

Mr. Karin: "Let me guess, does your problem involve a male counterpart?"

Samara: "Yes. I mean, not 'a counterpart'."

Mr. Karin: "And is that boy trouble for you or your love interest?"

(Fumbling, I look down at my feet again)

Mr. Karin: "I'm so sorry. Let's start from the beginning; tell me something about yourself. Who is the real Samara Laine?"

We have our initial sessions, and I greatly enjoy talking to Karin. I couldn't mention Aaron yet, I knew it wasn't the right time!

I paid my second visit the consecutive week and kept it low. He was trying to understand my nature, character, and background. He wanted to know my thought process.

On my third visit, I finally started feeling more comfortable talking to him...

Samara (my feet on the couch): "I don't know, Karin, but I feel like sometimes like I call trouble upon myself. I hate it when people tell me what to do! It's that one thing that I cannot stand in my life, but you know what the worst part is? They're mostly right, and I do end up taking the faulty steps, making the wrong decisions! And it makes me want to absolutely despise myself. People are taking authority over my life and I am unable to take any responsibility for it. I don't know what to do!"

Mr. Karin: "Do you think you're ready now?"

Samara: "Ready for what?"

Mr. Karin: "The real reason you needed this therapy? The boy who has been troubling you?"

Samara: "I never said... How do you know, Karin?"

Mr. Karin: "I can see through you, Samara; that's what I take your money for!"

Samara: "I don't understand!"

Mr. Karin: "You don't have to, my child. Tell me everything, from the very beginning till the exact moment your feet stepped in my house. *To help you*, I'd have to know everything that happened between you and that boy."

Samara: "It's very complicated, Karin!"

Mr. Karin: "Complicated sounds fun! Besides, we have all the time in the world. You don't have to finish the whole story today. We can continue it next time!"

Samara: "Well, it started when this friend I used to have got me two letters..."

I told Mr. Karin about the whole incident in great detail. I covered his letters, the rumours he spread, Valen's slap, my complaint to Brother Avi, and my defamation. I also mentioned his maniacal Instagram messages and blackmail to feed my parents those rumours.

Mr. Karin: "All this sounds pretty serious; why don't you call your friend in?"

Samara: "Who?"

Mr. Karin: "The one who waits for you outside every day!"

Samara: "Oh, Cher? I mean, Cherika. Yes, I will."

I go outside to fetch Cher.

Mr. Karin: "Why did you girls not do the police first? He has disturbed your peace and privacy for over five years. You waited until now to act?"

(We both looked at each other, then down at the floor, trying to find the right words before saying anything.)

Cher: "It's easier said than done, Doctor. You think this would have been so easy for us to do, but do you know the things she'd have to face then? Forget her, what about her parents? It's easier for a man to say this!"

Samara: "Cher, stop. You don't have to..."

Cher (agitated): "No, Summer. Doctor Karin here thinks it would have been so much easier if we had told our parents about it. The sole reason she continues to do this is because she hasn't complained yet, which makes her the culprit of the whole scenario and not that creepy stalker. I can't believe we take all these risks to come to this place and you end up victim-blaming us."

(Mr. Karin was smiling and watching us defend ourselves. I held Cher and asked her to sit back)

Samara: "See, Mr. Karin. You're right. We could have gone to the police. But, do you know how we live in a community? My parents would have to face something every day for a fault that wasn't theirs. Or worse, not even mine! Aaron's parents would have the high ground. They think their kid is so esteemed. But, in reality, he is a danger to us! I will be called things, called names that I have been hearing in the past, but now my parents will be there too."

Samara (taking a deep breath): "I'm unsure why I'm here, and I question your ability to help. I know you wouldn't advise him to change on his own. Nor would he listen, and involving his parents is unrealistic. And do you know what the worst feeling in the world is? Something I am faced with every day? The realization that I could have stopped this when I had the chance! When I could have been a little less of a trickster and simply said 'No' to his face. I live every day in the fear that somebody might call me *that word* again! I have trouble trusting men or falling in love, in the fear that if anything comes between us, what if they become like him? He has been following me since I came here. Pop culture romanticizes this, but it's bloody scary. *Even scarier, that I have gotten used to it!* Yes, we should have complained about this. The easy way to look at it is to think we didn't do it because we were casual about it. But, the harder truth will be to live with it, even after. This is no movie; this is life. And life has to go on even after the curtains roll."

After a deep and long pause...

Mr. Karin: "Go back home Samara and meet me the day after. I will work on your case and come up with what we must do."

Cher and I then leave at once from there with our hearts heavy.

Samara: "After the initial meeting, I really thought that he could help me, Cher. But this isn't going anywhere."

Cher: "Give it some time, sweetheart. I'm sure he'll come up with something. And if he doesn't, then we'll go directly talk to your mom and dad. You'll keep affecting your health for the rest of your life if you don't do anything about it. And don't suggest running away from the city. A thing like COVID will bring you back again. If not, he'll keep making different social accounts and messaging you."

Samara: "What if nobody believes me?"

Cher: "We never showed Brother Avi a screenshot. But he believed us. Our emotions and concerns were real. The same will happen now. Be honest, and the world will be with you, admit the things you did wrong and you will face their repercussions, and he will face him; we cannot let him go unchecked!"

Samara: "I tried doing that with Valen, Cher. I was honest even then, but he heard no word from me. What about that?"

Cher: "When will you start looking at the good side of things, baby girl? All that we can do is try. Surrender is not an option; persistence is the only choice."

Samara: "You're right. I cannot give up without even trying. Let's see how this goes..."

3 days later, at Mr. Karin's clinic, I slipped in unnoticed, since he would have expected me a day before. Still simmering over past discussions.

Samara: "I'm sorry, Mr. Karin; I shouldn't have spoken to you in that tone the other day."

Mr. Karin: "Oh, don't worry. At least I made you speak. Where's your friend? Call her in; I want to tell you both something very important!"

I called Cher and asked her to come inside. Mr. Karin had his whiteboard and markers ready; it seems like he is in the mood to give us a great deal of a lecture today.

Mr. Karin:

"EROTOMANIA"

"To be specific, the secondary form of Erotomania*. Your little friend Aaron is suffering from an uncommon psychological disorder. I'm worried about how much has it affected your boy. This often happens when someone hits rock bottom. They need something to link their rescue with. It may even be abstract, but most commonly, it's their love interest. The victim develops a parasocial relationship with the person, thought or idea. In this case of their one-sided, unrequited love, they treat the person as that whole relationship. Stalking or following the person is an extension of this. In their mind, it's just a reaction of recurring interactions. You mentioned that in college, he would text you something that felt like the continuation of a conversation. Normally, introductory texts start with a "Hey" or "Hi." But he was just messaging you as if you guys spoke all night. In the morning, he is apologizing for sleeping midway through the chat. Now, the scary part is that if we don't get this treated as early as possible, it might get even worse!"

Cher: "What do you mean, even worse?"

Mr. Karin: "I can't say anything. I've never met him. It would be unprofessional to comment based on just what my clients have told me. But we have to let his parents know about this so they can help him get the right medical attention. What's his name again?"

Samara: "Aaron. Aaron Shaw."

Mr. Karin (surprised): "Shaw? Wait! Is his father's name Yahya?"

Samara: "Yes, it is Dr Yahya Shaw."

Mr. Karin (hesitantly): "This can't be!"

Cher: "Why are you overreacting? Just tell us, what can't be?"

Mr. Karin: "Aaron Shaw is the son of Dr Yahya Shaw! He is one of the city's most reputed addiction psychiatrists. His medical career is inspiring to anyone who even dares to think of stepping on this field. He's been in the business longer than you kids would have breathed on Earth! But isn't it ironic? You moved out aspiring to fix the world, but what needed the most fixing was what was inside."

Samara: "I remember my mom telling me about Uncle Yahya and his profession, but I never thought it would be something so linked!"

Mr. Karin: "This is a great opportunity! Now that I know who the boy is, I can work on his case more closely. I will analyse public records and other sources to find out how he developed the condition. Knowing very well, that this can potentially sabotage my reputation, I am willing to do this for you Samara, my child. So don't you dare say that I never understood you or your pain, again. Dr Shaw is a good friend, he will not ignore this. He will definitely focus on getting his son treated."

Cher (doubtful): "Do you think Uncle Yahya would just believe you?"

Mr. Karin: "Parents from whichever profession are bound to get offended and affected when we mention their child. But we won't know unless we try!? Does Dr Yahya know his monk story?"

Samara: "Yes."

Mr. Karin: "Let me deduce the heat of the situation. I'll call him up; you girls stay here; I'll be back."

Mr. Karin left the room and came back 15 minutes later...

Mr. Karin (disappointed): "He is such a good old lad; it will be such a shock to him when he finds out about his son!"

Samara: "What happened, Mr. Karin? What did you talk about?"

Mr. Karin: "I couldn't make it sound like I called for a purpose. So, I started by mentioning my daughter's wedding. Then, I talked about his family."

Cher: "That's amazing! When is her wedding?"

Mr. Karin (smirking): "My daughter eloped a few years back and is now the mother of two. She lives in London."

Samara (amused): "Why did you lie to him?"

Mr. Karin: "It's common in our profession to forget personal life, my child. It's hard to keep up with your family affairs, let alone keep track of others. Dr Shaw was with me at the bar when I got drunk after my daughter had left."

Cher (giggling): "Well, that surely sounds like something! What did he say about Aaron?"

Mr. Karin: "This kid is great in academics. His parents, blinded by his talent, fulfil all his wishes. Recently, they've been worried. He doesn't talk to anyone, especially girls. Dr Shaw is concerned. He thinks the boy is too perfect. The real challenge? Dr. Yahya, despite being a highly qualified doctor, is Aaron's dad."

Cher (losing hope): "He wouldn't even believe you!"

Mr. Karin: "I tried to convince him that kids these days have a duality of nature because they are so afraid of their parents. They are ideal before us, but a totally different person with their friends. He said his son isn't like that. He is too innocent for the world, and people keep poking him, and it's hard for them to take care of him from afar! I have worked on people who show duality, but this guy is good."

Samara: "Welcome to our world!"

Mr. Karin: "I have a plan. I'll send you a letter mail explaining the whole thing; it will be addressed to your mother. Can't risk leaving any digital footprints. Read it as instructions, and follow everything as the dates mentioned. (Looking at Cher) Drop me a text when you guys are ready. We have to expose this guy."

Samara: "We'll do as you say."

Mr. Karin: "Let me summarize this out loud, he was rejected at a young age, got bullied by his love interest, and revenge-plotted against her. Then became very spiritual. He blackmailed to show fake pictures to your parents. Dr Yahya's wife doesn't think highly of you.

After all that, he has been messaging and following you. Am I correct?"

Samara (anxious): "Now that you say it, it makes me sound really bad!"

Mr. Karin: "The spiritual angle scares me. We don't know what kind of people he's been with..."

Samara: "Should we be scared, Mr. Karin?"

Mr. Karin: "No girls. I'll work and gather as much information as I can. Drop your mother's name and address on this paper, and you both can leave..."

We leave from there and think of nothing, but what has been explained.

Him living his life in his head and then reflecting on it in real life. That's really strange and frightening. To even think of a thing like that shakes up my whole body with fear.

A few days later, the three of us meet at a café.

Ayo: "Do you think we should try talking to Valen? I mean, he was there through it, and he can help us share his side too!"

Samara: "I'm not sure, man. I haven't spoken to him for over two years now! Also, the circumstances weren't too great for me to reconnect with him."

Cher: "The worst he can say is 'No'. You should give it a shot! We'll never know if you don't even try."

Samara: "This is really awkward, guys. How do I start? Should I pick up from where we left off, or just pretend as though nothing ever happened... Talk to him like a good old friend, seek direct help or sound as if I wanna start things afresh!?"

Ayo: "Wait, don't stress yourself so much; you have a lot to be stress over already. Let me try talking to him first. Cher can burst out any time before him, so I should do it. We will know his stance and then ask him if he is comfortable speaking to you."

This being the better plan, Ayo talks to him that night and briefly explains the plan, asking if he is willing to be a part.

The next day...

Ayo (displeased): "He isn't in for it."

Samara: "I told you guys. Let's not push this anymore."

Cher: "What did he say?"

Ayo: "I explained everything to him, from the false story to Aaron's stalking. I asked him to speak for us, but he denied it, saying he wanted to leave that life behind. He also apologized to you, Summer, for his past words. He misses you and your companionship."

Samara: "I don't blame him. I would probably do the same if I were him. This is all our mess."

Cher: "Wasn't he the one who played a significant part in creating this mess?"

Samara: "He moved on, Cher. We cannot force somebody to do something we want. Aaron gave him a hard time too; the last thing we should do is make someone go through it over again. Nobody signs up for that! I have had nights where I couldn't sleep, and somewhere I know that Valen would have gone through those as well."

Ayo: "One more thing, he said he wished you would have confessed your feelings when it was the right time, not when everything had gone downhill."

Samara: "It's too late for all that now; I guess we have to plan on getting rid of Aaron for now."

A few days later...

There's the postman at the gate with a mail, exactly as Mr. Karin had described. I rush to take it and run to my room under the sheets to open it. It's a five-page blueprint of his plan. He called it our "instruction manual."

"

Dear Samara,

My child, after working on this case, I cannot imagine the trauma you must have suffered because of this boy. Not to forget, calling out your extremely irresponsible reaction to it. What I am about to ask you to do must never be recommended as a Mental Health Professional, but I'm suggesting to do this as a confidante and a friend. Dr. Yahya would never believe us unless he sees things for himself.

So, hear me carefully and do exactly as I say. On 25th August, I will be coming to your area; you need to bring Aaron to this location. . .

"

-end of chapter-

The Story of Aaron

Aaron Shaw, the youngest son of Dr Yahya and Mrs. Noreen Shaw, and brother of Avram Shaw (our beloved Brother Avi), was born into a family of geniuses, Aaron did not excel in studies from the get-go. Brother Avi was born a prodigy, a scholar, and a gold medallist in Math. There wasn't a year until his undergrad that he wouldn't have secured top scores. Mrs. Noreen Shaw was a social worker, the most educated among her sisters. She was known for her work in literary clubs and teaching in community schools. Dr. Yahya was a well-known psychiatrist in town. He specialized in severe addiction cases and consulted even celebrities and politicians in the area.

They also strongly believed in religion and astrology. They took Brother Avi to their family priest before major life events. But since Aaron wasn't a living replication of Brother Avi, they had always been worried about him. Despite being a well-respected and educated family, all did not work for Aaron. In the initial years of his childhood, he had been heavily monitored by his parents. He had no free will. He had to get the scores his parents prescribed. He couldn't buy anything for himself, unlike kids his age. He couldn't even talk to his classmates or be friends with them, without their approval. Only the kids who he would go to common classes with were "permitted" to be his friends.

Everything had to go through them. They wouldn't physically harm him, but their verbal disapproval and disappointment did the deed for him.

They imposed restrictions on everything. They believed it protected their child from social evils. This upbringing shattered his self-esteem. They saw fun and laughing around the streets with friends as *fatherless* behaviour.

One day, when he was around 11 years old, some of his friends had come over and his father had recently discovered the test scores that he had been hiding in his bag. Dr Yahya got furious and scolded him before his friends. His friends, being braindead, found this whole thing funny and spread the word in their class. The kids from his class then started bullying him and calling him all kinds of names. 'Sweetheart' and 'Pussycat Doll' were among the gentle ones, associating his 'non-manliness' before his father as a consequence of his sexual homogeneity and called out his inability to rebel against them.

For the longest time, all he wished for was to run away from his home and parents, to live a life where he wasn't just "their" child.

One day, he was in classroom solving math problems when he dropped his eraser on the floor while working. It was just then that a girl walked by as he rose; his face got stuck in her skirt, pulling it up.

The girl misunderstood the accident and instantly blew it as though he were trying to peep in. She screamed out loud, panicking. Aaron constantly apologized to her for it.

"MA'AM, AARON IS TRYING TO SMELL INTO MY SKIRT!!!"

All the teachers from around the place rushed in to see all this chaos. Aaron, along with the girl, had been called to the principal's office.

The principal was this wonderful lady who actually heard Aaron clarify his part. How this was just an accident, and he was deeply apologetic about it.

The girl, however, was convinced that all this was just a cover-up and he was caught in his intended act. She wouldn't accept his apology and she further complained about how she had seen him staring at her distastefully before.

The principal gave him a warning and made him write 'Apology Letters' to both her and the girl. She wanted to believe that this was an accident, but the girl was displeased by this impermanent solution.

She was the daughter of a very influential man around the city and a teen diva herself. All the boys in her class, trying to impress the girl, collectively announced a social boycott against him. Aaron, on the other hand, who was just a "scaredy-cat" before, was now also an offender. He had become an outcast, and now it was just too 'uncool' for anyone to even talk to him.

Being completely unaware of all this, his mom further threatened to send him off to boarding school if he did not do well in his studies. The burden of carrying both the expectations of his parents and the social exclusion from school had increasingly become bothersome to him. He began lying to his parents. He never even confessed to them about being bullied and getting this mental exile from his peers. His father was extremely strict and unapproachable when came to expressing anything except for dismay or disapproval. His brother and mother were also mostly busy with their work. He never felt loved or even accepted by anyone.

It was around this time that he had found solace within himself as his sole confidante. He would harm himself in isolation, both physically and emotionally, but every time, he stopped; blamed, and hated himself even more for not being strong enough. He would cry himself to sleep only to dream of not waking up ever again. He was extremely afraid of his dad, whom he felt never loved him, and his brother wouldn't consider him. His self-hatred grew making him feel that he was unworthy of love.

He eventually hypothesized a version of him that suited his parents and then started projecting that image. Lying about his scores on tests, learning editing for his certificates, pretending to be well-mannered before everyone, covering up for everything, and making the best attempts to ensure that his parents and teachers never met. And for the greater good, it worked!

His parents started treating him with more respect than ever before.

In his classes, he wouldn't really interact with anyone and hardly have any friends even in his neighbourhood. At the age of around 13, his father had gotten the opportunity to move to a bigger house in the city.

Aaron did not care about it much, but to his surprise, people in the area had a much greater acceptance of him. Since he was now a teenager, his parents dropped the monitoring. He had found a playground around the house where boys of different ages gathered together to play football, and every evening he made it a point to go there!

This was where he met Ayona, his immediate neighbour for the first time, who later introduced him to Samara and Cherika. He would usually catch all three of them together across the streets, but one day Samara was crossing and upon making eye contact, smiled at him.

.

.

For the first time in his life, he felt recognized.

Until then, he had killed his self-worth to a level that being noticed by anybody had not even been a possibility.

Every evening, Samara would smile at him passing by as a pleasantry. He saw hope in her, making him want to be better, to be a gentleman. He timed his crossings to encounter her. He had started following her routine, her habits, knowing the people she met, and the places she hung out in. In his mind, he built scenarios for their exchanges. This make-believe grew, especially after being bullied. When he'd come home and share the happenings of his day with a pretentious Samara. He didn't want her to see his true self. He aimed to show her a different Aaron. The Aaron who fought back. The Aaron who wasn't an outcast. The one who seemed to not care. Care about anything that lured the hip teens of his batch. He wanted to be the Aaron meant just for Samara.

He felt that she could take him out of his misery...

After a year, they finally spoke during the festival celebration. Ayo and Cher were away, and Samara was alone with the kids. Aaron aimed to pick up their last conversation. But this time, he heard her story, for this time his curiosity sparked. He wanted to be with her all the time. He craved to know everything about her; the shows she watched, the books she read, her favourite things, her subjects, her colour preferences, and her friends.

He wasn't a stalker by intent, but he became one by his actions.

On one of the days, his friends caught him speaking to himself. Upon confronting, he pretended to speak on the phone with his 'girlfriend' Samara. At first, his friends doubted it because of his speculated 'preferences.' However, his sincerity convinced them. Then, they noticed Samara smiling at him one day. This eased their doubts entirely. Aaron's social standing suddenly improved, thanks to *someone* claiming him. His story became believable to his parents after years of convicted repetition. Life was looking up for him. He had become a skilled con-artist.

Then one day, Valen joined their football gang and discovered his secrets.

Valen and Samara's friendship had always deeply affected Aaron, and all that he ever wanted to do was break their friendship.

The first ever blow of betrayal for him was when he saw both, Samara and Valen, chilling outside her house. He felt cheated by her for flirting with another guy. This was the downside of him being lovelorn, turning it into a manic obsession and eventually commoditizing Samara. It was no longer his love for Samara that kept him going; it was a question of pride because his motive for living this new life had been gambled by a foreign force, and it was this very survival instinct that was now at stake, that gave rise to his eventual erotomanic tendencies...

Chapter 6:
Closure

24th August 2021...

"It's been raining cats and dogs for the past hour, and I had come to get the groceries on my bike. I try my hardest to escape the heavy pouring rain, but the raindrops on my specs are blinding my eyes. There's no choice but to wait out here in the rain! I park my bike at a shop's corner to remove my glasses, still standing by for the rain to stop. My myopic eyes blur my vision again, I take them off to wipe them clean. As I wear them back again, I sense something eerily suspicious."

My fears grow loud as I look around. I bawl myself all over hastily, feeling the sounds of all my breaths; I see no one...

I understand at once. It's him...

It couldn't be anyone else but him!

He who breathes in my shadows,

Follows me like the breeze.

Guards me like a canine...

Wherever I go, whatever I do, he's right there standing, waiting for me...

He walks as I walk, and stops when I halt. There isn't a footprint of mine without his behind it.

My footsteps have lost their sound; they have become in sync with his!

It's weird; there's a strange security even in my solitude, that I am never really alone. But the rest of the time, it feels just as haunting because I Am Never Alone.

He is Always there. Everywhere...

The raindrops lower, I take my bicycle and rush out. At that very moment, I saw him coming out from behind the other shop, taking his bicycle.

He is still behind me when I stop under a tree.

Samara: "Aaron, I can see you there; why don't you just come out and talk to me?"

Aaron (looking around and defending): "What do you mean? It was raining, and I was at the grocery store too."

Samara (after a deep sigh): "How are you?"

Aaron (confused): "Who, me?"

Samara: "Who else is here for me to talk to?"

Aaron (nervously looking around): "You never really spoke to me, so I wondered."

Samara: "Exactly, Aaron, I've never been good to you, or even spoken to you, so why do you still follow me or expect anything from me?"

Aaron: "You wouldn't understand. You have never truly loved anyone in your life."

Samara (offended): "That hurts, wow. Anyway, the rain is coming down; I must leave..."

Aaron: "No, wait. We can talk..."

Samara: "Cher and Ayo would be expecting me."

Aaron: "We can talk sometime."

Samara: "Meet me tomorrow; I'll tell you the place."

Aaron (shocked): "Really?"

Aaron (still processing): "I mean, you don't plan on pranking me, right?"

Samara: "Oh no, really. There is something I need to speak to you about."

Aaron: "Do you promise?"

Samara: "Yes, I promise, I mean mostly. Peach Tree Alley, Street 20. Be there at 6; I don't like to wait."

I say this and leave from there to catch up with Ayo and Cher, and then immediately switch off my phone.

Samara: "I've called him to Peach Tree Alley. I hope everything works out this time..."

Ayo: "Fingers crossed, it will work. Don't worry."

Cher: "This time we have the support of an older, wiser man!"

Next day, 25th August, 2021...

I reach Peach Tree Alley at 6 and see Aaron waiting for me there; he had probably arrived 15 minutes earlier, smelling like somebody, straight outta 'Kobra Deodorant' commercial.

Aaron (smiling): "Hi!"

Samara (awkwardly): "Hey, Aaron."

Aaron: "Why did you want to meet me?"

Samara: "Yeah, I just wanted to clear the air between us and also understand a lot of the things you have been doing."

He looked anxious, almost unconfident to look me in the eye.

Aaron: "I just wanted to know one thing: do you have a boyfriend?"

Samara: "Don't you know by now? You have all of my friends' list!"

Aaron: "What? I mean, what do you mean?"

Samara: "Nothing, and yes I do, back in college. But anyway, that's not the point; the point is, why have you been doing all this? Following me everywhere, texting around my friends, blackmailing me?! Do you think all this would ever make me love you?"

Aaron (with loud conviction): "Summer, you don't understand! I love you. I have loved you all my life. My love for you is the only thing that I have ever known, ever felt. I can't sleep at night because I'm scared that you might be with me in my dreams, but when I wake up, you are no longer there."

Samara: "Okay, okay, calm down, you don't need to simp around. I understand what you're saying. You have loved me your whole life and all, but I am in a committed relationship. What do you expect me to do? I cannot break my relationship with the LOML just because you like me, right? That'll be extremely unfair to him."

Aaron: "What's his name?"

Samara: "Armand. Armand Rinaldi."

Aaron: "That guy can never love you the way I do, Summer."

Samara: "Please, can you just call me Samara? Also, it's not a competition between you and him. It's about who I wanna be with!"

Aaron: "I will love you always; you will see how he leaves you alone one day, but I won't ever think about that!"

Samara: "No, that's not true. Armand loves me a lot and would be extremely affected if I ever told him something like this!"

Aaron: "Yeah, the same way Reece and Valen did, and then left you to live alone?"

Samara (enraged): "Don't you dare!"

Aaron: "It's been more than five years now, Samara, and you can clearly see who stuck around and who didn't."

Samara: "Maintain your boundaries, Aaron. You cannot just say anything to me. It's a relief they left when it was time for them to go. At least, they respected my decision to not be a part of their lives anymore, unlike you who have stuck on me like a fly."

Aaron: "You seriously don't see all that I can do for you; I would even kill for you, Summer!"

Samara (bursting): "It's fu*king SAMARA for you, you asshole! What do you think of yourself? You could kill for me? And why exactly would I want to spend the rest of my life with a murderer? Earn some respect for yourself, dude. What do you think you will get from all this? Me? Definitely not!"

Aaron (calmly): "I will care for you; I will keep you happy!"

Samara (irritated): "For crying out loud, get a real job!"

Samara: "Okay, picture this: in all your Instagram messages, you wanted a chance, right? A chance to speak to me? I'm giving you the chance; come, speak to me, and have an insightful conversation with me."

"Go ahead, please speak!"

"I'm dying to hear what you have to say to me, Aaron!"

"What do you even know about me? About my dreams, my interests? What are you willing to do for me?"

Aaron (stammering): "I know that you like photography!"

Samara: "When I was 15, I hadn't picked up the camera since then. Next question."

Aaron: "How has your college been?"

Samara: "It's been pathetic; I got scolded in my PM class for not adding the right amount of ease after converting the fish dart to a style line. Still can't get the ditch stitch of my bias-bound seam right and have wasted over three swatches until now. RJ is a real pain because I did not present him with the sketches he asked for. I haven't started compiling my portfolio yet, and people from my batch have already secured their internships. I've been left far, far behind in the things that my contemporaries have achieved. I have no idea how to cope with all this!"

Aaron: "I'm sure you'll be great; you are amazing at your work, and I have full faith in you!"

Samara: "Oh really? And exactly what makes you think my work is amazing? Can you mention what you like about it?"

Aaron: "I have seen your Behance; you have curated it very well."

Samar: "It isn't updated, and it isn't as great as the others. I don't like it. Which project did you like the most?"

Aaron: "The one... which has some cool stuff... with all the collages and some animations."

Samara: "a. That's a mood board."

"b. It's a digital illustration, not an animation. Also, which one are you referring to exactly?"

Aaron: "That doesn't matter; you will be all right in your academics."

Samara: "You clearly have no idea about my professional life. Let's talk about my personal life. I have another problem: the girls I am around have treated me badly, but I have learned my lesson and really want to be better in my future friendships."

Aaron: "Tell me their names; I'll teach them a lesson!"

Samara: "No, no, it's not their problem. I fell into the trap of their harsh ways of bullying. I need to change myself and make myself a little more steadfast about the people I spend my time with."

Aaron: "No, you're perfect just the way you are! You don't have to change anything about yourself."

Samara: "Am I? But aren't you the one who convinced people that I was a wh*re? (I could feel that he was losing his calm.) Like, do you even know the meaning of the word? You ruined my entire image down to a characterless woman who sleeps with a random bunch of men?! Do you seriously even know what this could have caused in my life, had people given you a little more attention!? All that time, you just saw me laughing around guys and thought I was sleeping with them!? How shallow can you be!? And you expect me to love someone who was the source of this bullcrap without any concrete evidence, apart from some morphed images? Picture this, one fine day we actually end up dating each other, wouldn't I always be scared that if I ever left you, you'd spread an even bigger, more scandalous story about me than this? 'Samara dated Aaron for money and left' or 'she was found cheating on him with another man!' or even better, 'Your girl is back on sale, 6999/- a night'!"

Aaron: "No, I'm sorry. I made a mistake, but that's just how it looked back then; and why I told everybody about it that way."

Samara: "Tell me? What if you catch me cheating on you with someone who makes me happier?"

Aaron: "I will kill anyone who even dares to come close to you..."

Samara: "No, I'm equally to blame for cheating on you. Maybe you couldn't keep me happy, and I lost interest. I found some other guy, and I'm now attracted to him! Would you care to listen to my side of the story?"

Aaron: "Don't push it, Summer!"

Samara: "Maybe I don't find you physically attractive, and I want to explore other possibilities."

Aaron: "Stay within your limits, Summer!"

Summer: "After all, I should have the choice of tasting all the fish from the sea, right?"

Aaron immediately held and slapped me...

Aaron: (burning with rage) "HOW DARE YOU!?"

Samara (after taking a moment from recovery): "Exactly, Aaron, this exactly. You and I have nothing in common; we have no goals that align. You don't know shit about me, my personality, my life, and neither do I. All you want is to keep me captive and just talk about some love bullshit!? The worst part is, even if I ever love you and things fall apart between us, you would still cage me like a prisoner! Have you ever thought, what after it? How will you provide for my dreams or keep me happy? Any ambitions of yours that you wish to pursue? Or am I just a possession for you and your dreams that are far far from reality!??? Have you ever really even thought about me that way?"

Aaron gasps at me and chokes me, holding me by the neck.

Aaron: "SHUT UP! Just shut up! I will kill every man who comes near you and know that if I can love you so passionately, I can kill you too. ANY DAY! You have not seen the madness I hold for you! I will destroy every guy you bag your eyes on, just the way I did with Valen. What do you think? You can make me feel this way every time and just get away with it? (waving his fingers across my face, while I am still struggling to breathe) I could make you mine this instant, but this love... My love for you makes me want you to love me instead. Love me the way I do or I will never stop trying, and I don't care about another living soul! Why don't you understand this, baby? I NEED you..."

'KEEP YOUR HANDS OFF HER!!' screamed a strangely familiar voice.

Just the very instant, Mr. Karin emerged from behind, alongside Dr Yahya, his wife, Cher, Ayo, and Valen. Mr. Karin had told them everything, and he had called Cher and Ayo. Cher had spoken to Valen and called him too, as he was one of the witnesses.

Aaron saw them and jerked me away; his grip on my neck was so strong that it left imprints on my neck, again.

Dr Yahya came forward and smacked him across the face.

Mr. Karin: "You heard him, Dr Yahya; he has been in love with Samara and has been following her for the past five years!"

Dr Yahya and Aunt Noreen were astonished. The Earth beneath them crumbled. Dr Yahya held Aaron by his collar and screamed, "How did you even dare to talk to a girl like that?"

Valen went ahead to stop him from punching him again.

Mr. Karin: "Control your anger, Dr. This isn't how we should tackle this situation."

Dr. Yahya dropped his collar. With his voice cracking, he said, "I took pride in raising you to be the greatest of men. But you turned out to be a monster. What did you say again, you would kill anyone who comes your way or you kill this poor girl?"

Mr. Karin: "Doctor, we must take Aaron and speak with him first; I request you to control yourself. I know how stressful all this can be for you. But no amount of abuse can solve any of this!"

Aunt Noreen: "This is personal, Mr. Karin; this cannot happen! (turning to Aaron) You lied to us all these years; wouldn't you always tell us that you wanted to be a monk, Aaron? What is all this, then?"

Aaron was looking away, unable to process everything that had happened. Cher and Ayo held me from both sides as we saw all this.

Mr. Karin: "Doctor, please hear me. I have been studying the boy's case for over a few weeks now, and I want you to listen to me before you take any action against this boy!"

Valen: "Listen, everyone, this really isn't the right place! Let's go somewhere inside and talk!"

Mr. Karin: "The kid is right! Let's not create a scene out here; a lot of people need to face the consequences of their past actions! (Mr. Karin gave me a grave look.)"

We all proceeded to Dr Yahya's house, and Mr. Karin had called my mother too. Valen came near me to ask, "Are you okay?" I nodded. He wouldn't look at me during this entire chaos.

We all sat in his living area, and Aaron was sent away to his room.

Mr. Karin: (Looking at Dr. Yahya and Aunt Noreen) "I want you to listen to me very carefully. We wouldn't want to not give the benefit of the doubt to the boy, but these girls have certain confessions to make. It's unfair to ignore the boy's side. We don't want a 'he said, she said' situation. (Turning to my mother) I'm Karin Sharmon, a retired LMHC. I offer therapy consultations to people in need. A few weeks ago, your daughter came to me. She shared her problems. After our exchanges, I found out they stemmed from a boy. He'd been pursuing her for a long time. He even tried to choke her when she rejected him. She never talked to you about this because she feared being greatly scolded by you and losing her independence. That's the first point. However, these girls did try to have a bit of an intervention with Mrs. Noreen." (Looking at Aunt Noreen)

Aunt Noreen: "We had no idea what these kids had been cooking all those years; please watch your words here, Mr. Karin."

Mr. Karin: "As I said, everyone in this room has consequences to face for their actions. So please listen to me before you say anything."

(Looking at my mom)

"Starting with you, Mrs. Laine. Your daughter has been facing this all these years, hiding away something so serious from you, because she couldn't confide in you! Do you know what she said when I asked her why she came to me and did not go to the police to file a case of severe stalking? (imitating my voice) 'Mr. Karin, my parents will know!' She fears her own parents, her supposed protectors. How will you ever fight social evils when you can't even stand up before your own parents? Because she would be scolded?"

"Please, can someone give me a glass of water? This is going to take for a very long time!" (Ayo rushed to the kitchen to get him a glass of water)

(Turning to Mrs. and Dr. Shaw) The same goes for you two! I am extremely sorry, Dr. Yahya. I am talking to you in this language, but this is about the life of my daughter-like client. Do you know why Aaron wore this mask, over all these years? Because he was afraid of you! You always pressured him for the greatness he never possessed that he ultimately convinced you of what you wanted! You did not expect to raise a good man; you expected a trophy son who could bear the pride of your high esteem. You know, his harmless affection for this certain female grew obsessive because it was his way of escaping reality, from this burden of expectations. He could never accept 'no' for an answer, as the girl was never in question. What was in question was his escape from reality, and that urge doesn't die through years and years! Please sit with him and recognize that he needs help. I've concluded your boy has severe paranoid delusions and erotomania. These issues might stem from social exclusion, childhood trauma, or lack of validation. He believed Samara was doing everything for him. He thought she was secretly messaging him, too shy to make their relationship public. I am sure you would have also witnessed him talking to himself.

Dr. Yahya (unsure, looking at his wife): "No, he doesn't!"

Aunt Noreen (interrupting): "He does. I thought he'd made friends in college. I would hear him speaking in his room since the lockdown. But, one day, I was cleaning the front room and saw his phone near the TV stand. I did not put much thought into it because we had a landline or it could be a Zoom call as well, but thinking back now, the landline isn't in his room."

Mr. Karin: "That's right, that's probably his dialogue with his *partner* Samara, where he might be taking some serious life advice from her."

Mr. Karin further disclosed the whole story before his parents, and the rest of us contributed to the parts we witnessed firsthand.

Dr and Mrs. Shaw were sitting extremely uncomfortably, still trying to process every instance. This had been a real shocker for them too...

Cher: "But what do we do now!? Will Samara ever be free from his toxic advances?"

Aunt Noreen: "You girls needn't worry about that! (turning to me and holding my hand) I promise you, I will make sure that you never hear from him again. I apologize for the way I might have behaved with you before, but I will keep my eyes open now and not be blinded by my pride."

Dr. Yahya: "Yes, my daughter. We will not let Aaron get to you and have him treated by the best in business! Thank you, Mr. Karin, for helping these girls and helping me!"

(Turning to the other side)

Mr. Karin: "I hope you give him the best care and do not do anything to him that scars him any further. All he needs is genuine love and humility for what he is and not what you expect him to be, Dr Yahya. I would have offered you my services, but I think I'll have my biases because Samara is my dearest."

Dr Yahya: "I understand."

Mr. Karin: "We parents forget our kids are human. They have their flaws and personalities, different from the ones we impose on them! (turning to me) I hope your therapy was worth it, Samara. Make sure you feel good about yourself and do a little less childish stuff! (jokingly)

I'll share your invoice! You are a grown woman now, feel free to connect with me whenever. I mustn't overstay or someone would definitely slap me. I will take you guys a leave."

After a much-required break, Mr. Karin leaves, and Dr Yahya accompanies to see him off.

Aunt Noreen still looks shocked.

My mom came up to me and said, "My child, we need to have a heart-to-heart discussion today!" she left me with my friends here. Although I expected her to be angrier than this, I think what Mr. Karin said, worked.

"Hey, listen, I'm really sorry!"

I turn around and see Valen standing. "I shouldn't have trusted Aaron or those pictures back then."

Samara: "That's fine, Valen."

Valen: "We used to be the best of friends; I guess I was really shocked to see you with Reece."

Samara: "Yes, Valen, we were. And I am extremely grateful that you came, but I think we must cherish our old friendship as it was and not let anything ruin that beautiful memory."

Valen (face turning tense): "What do you mean?"

Samara: "I mean to say to you that we have lived a life after everything happened. It's nice if we just stay connected, but maybe not the way we used to be! Being around each other would only keep reminding us of the past over and over again and not let us move ahead, you know!"

We both chuckled, and all of us left his house. Valen took my word for it and respected my decision. After all, he understood the turmoil of being around someone you used to like and getting affected by their actions!

Cher, Ayo, and I group-hugged each other.

"It's over, girls!" I could feel myself heavily tearing up.

Cher: "Yes, it finally is..."

Samara: "I could have never done it without you guys! You both are angels to me."

Ayo: "And there's not a thing that we wouldn't have done for you! You are our baby..."

Before leaving, Aunt Noreen assured that Aaron wouldn't bother me. I made her promise not to punish him and hear him out.

I went home and told Momma everything I had kept a secret until that moment. This included issues about our privacy and social security. I shared how we had been teased and violated by both known and unknown elders since childhood.

The next day...

At 5 p.m., I went down the street for a walk; both Cher and Ayo had gone out with their families. I looked around and took a deep breath...

I was alone...

Epilogue

Dr. Yahya handled the situation very well after we all left that day. He and his wife decided to speak bluntly about all their mistakes and also the things Aaron had done. He took a week off and the family went for a holiday. Brother Avi joined them from there and after returning, they ensured to get him the best professional help. This time, they made sure to give him the space he needed and also made him feel loved. What Mr. Karin had told him, worked really well and he wanted to ensure that Aaron felt validated by him for being him.

After about a year, since Dr. Yahya was already 55, he took early retirement from his clinic and moved to the hills, where he could give more time to his family and worked with online consultations.

Aunt Noreen kept her promise and Aaron never approached me again...

Mr. Karin is the greatest old lad! He keeps sending me dad jokes every once in a while.

Ayo proceeded to pursue her Master's in Dentistry. Cher finished to degree in Biotechnology and worked at a Patenting company. Both in their own stable and extremely beautiful relationships...

As for me, I am here... Happy and mostly, undisturbed...

Characters

1. **Samara Laine** (as Summer) – The Protagonist
2. **Ayona Kain** (as Ayo) – As Summer's close friend and partner-in-crime
3. **Cherika Shiki** (as Cher) – As Summer's close friend and partner-in-crime
4. **Valen Moore** - Summer's close friend and older love interest
5. **Aaron Shaw** - The Antagonist
6. **Avram Shaw** (Brother Avi) - Aaron's brother
7. **Nico** – Summer's old friend
8. **Kai** – Summer's old friend
9. **Reece** - Summer's Situationship
10. **Mr. Karin Sharmon** - The LMHC (Licensed Mental Health Counsellor) therapist
11. **Samara's mother**
12. **Aunt Noreen Shaw** - Aaron's mother
13. **Dr. Yahya Shaw** - Aaron's father
14. **Avasa** –Summer's Childhood friend
15. **Danish** – Avasa's Brother
16. **Khalil** - A random dude from college
17. **Yoshi** – Summer's innocent friend from school
18. **Yana** – Summer's friend from the Costume Design Team
19. **Jude** - Valen's younger brother
20. **Armond Rinaldi** – Summer's Fake Boyfriend

Disclaimer: Mental Health

EROTOMANIA: A delusional disorder involving unrequited love.

The aim of the novel is not to use the effects of a psychological disorder to extract plot-related comedic relief from the story but to explore the impacts and grow awareness of its consequences on both the person suffering from the psychiatric disabilities and the abusee. It is also worth noting that this piece has not been written by a subject matter expert and must be dealt with through these lenses only!

This novel also does not aim to villainize any individual or entity by its medium or distribution.

SO, WHAT REALLY IS EROTOMANIA?

Erotomania is a rare delusional disorder characterised by an individual's persistent belief that another person is in love with them, despite a lack of evidence to support this claim. The target of the delusion may be a celebrity, politician, or other high-status person, but it can also be a random stranger, acquaintance, or even someone who has died.

SYMPTOMS:

The core symptom of erotomania is an unshakable belief that another person is secretly in love with the individual. This delusion often leads to problematic behaviours such as:

- Sending letters, emails, or gifts to the target.
- Making persistent phone calls or visits to the target.
- Believing that the target is sending secret messages through gestures, media, or coded communication.
- Stalking or harassing the target, sometimes to the point of arrest.
- Feeling jealous due to a belief that the target is unfaithful or in love with others.

Classified as primary or secondary:

Primary erotomania exists alone without comorbidities, has a sudden onset, and has a chronic course. **Secondary erotomania** is found alongside other mental disorders like schizophrenia and often includes additional symptoms such as hallucinations and grandiose ideas.

CAUSES AND RISK FACTORS:

The exact causes of erotomania are not fully understood, but several factors may contribute:

- Genetics and family history of psychiatric disorders
- Underlying mental health conditions, such as schizophrenia, bipolar disorder, or delusional disorder.
- Substance abuse, including alcoholism and drug use.
- Severe loneliness, low self-esteem, or ego deficits following a major loss.
- Unsatiated urges related to homosexuality or narcissism.
- Brain abnormalities, like heightened temporal lobe asymmetry,

Erotomania appears to be slightly more common in women, but it may be more dangerous in men due to an increased risk of violent and stalker-like behaviours.

Treatment for erotomania typically involves a combination of therapy and medication to address the underlying psychosis and delusional symptoms.

- Psychotherapy

- including cognitive-behavioural therapy (CBT) to challenge delusional beliefs

- Treatment for any co-occurring mental health conditions, such as mood stabilisers for bipolar disorder, is important.

- Antipsychotic medications

In rare cases where the individual poses a serious threat to themselves or others, involuntary hospitalisation may be necessary. Erotomania can lead to dangerous, even deadly, outcomes if left untreated, including stalking, harassment, and violence.

Source:
1. Erotomania by GoodTherapy (https://www.goodtherapy.org/blog/psychpedia/erotomania)

2. Erotomania by Healthline (https://www.healthline.com/health/erotomania)

3. Erotomania: When Love Is a Delusion by Psychology Today (https://www.psychologytoday.com/us/blog/psych-unseen/201904/erotomania-when-love-is-delusion)

4. What is erotomania? by WebMD (https://www.webmd.com/mental-health/what-is-erotomania)
5. Erotomania by Wikipedia

   (https://en.wikipedia.org/wiki/Erotomania)

Acknowledgements

I would like to dedicate all my life's work to my absolutely amazing parents, Mr. Madhusudan Naik and Mrs. Jema Mani Naik, who have been taking care of me and my Gen-Z impulsive life choices, from pursuing Fashion Design to working a corporate job and then moving into writing. Standing strong with me, and not really being able to oppose much because I am so stubborn (younger-sibling benefits).

My brother Vivek Naik, who did not speak with me much, at least until I became a writer and also for greatly shaping my childhood and being my only mirror of morality.

My siblings, who have shown immense support in every stage of life and have also contributed to giving just the right advice at the right time. They mean nothing less than the world to me: Harry Naik, Nikita Das, Evleena Naik, Hitesh Jerai, Priyanka Pragya, Sovan Kumar, and Anmol Sinku!

Mr. Guru Charan Naik, Mrs. Neelkamal Naik, Mrs. Kavita Sinku, Mr. Birendra Sinku, the late Ms. Golanti Naik, the late Mr. Sarat Chandra Naik, and the late Mrs. Parbati Naik, who have taken great care of me and cherished my being from the moment I breathed on the surface of the Earth.

My amazing circle of friends, who have actually been with me through thick and thin, making my life more enjoyable, moments more memorable, and my belief in human connections much stronger! My school friends: Arpita, Aastha, Sana, Gloriana, Vaibhavi, Aakanksha, Monali, Saket, Rajat, Abhishek, Kalash, and Aadi. My college friends, Aditi, Nandu, Namrata, Madhumita and Sakshi; my greatest support and friendly advisor, Krishna; my super helpful and fun seniors, Harsh sir, Amit sir, and Prajwal; and my lovely juniors, Nimish, Onkar, and Nancy <3!

Special mention to Apoorva and Shreya for inspiring the beautiful characters of Cher and Ayo, and living with me parts of the story (that were true).

Cannot speak enough about these people who have been with me through both the good and bad parts of life and still stand strong! Lots of friendships have been with me throughout my life; the rest have given me the greatest lessons, with every reason to cherish and treasure them forever!

Beyond anything else, a huge shoutout to my roots in the suburbs of Bhilai for being my comfort place! I would despise the whole city for not being 'cool' enough back in childhood, but I crave going back to the city more than ever now! The countless number of memories the place has given me; every street in sector 10 has a story hidden for me, and I owe my everything to this place for being so nice to me in a bittersweet way!

Note from the Author

This story is totally fictional! (Except for the parts that are not!) The book's intend is not to villainize anybody, and total maturity is also expected from everyone reading.

I would deeply like to thank my stalker for finally growing up in life. For the past 3 years I haven't heard anything from him have been the happiest! Hoping for nothing but the best for him, no more hate at all. A heartfelt gratitude for giving me a story worthy of turning into a book. Despite taking real-life resemblance, more than ninety per cent of the story is how it played out in my head.

This has been among the scariest parts of my life, with some sort of similar tonality as seen in the lives of others around me, too! All the characters being exemplified versions of the real selves. There were times while writing this novel, that I was forced to accept my behavioural patterns, and how in certain situations I did not act like the bigger person and unintentionally (or not) left loopholes that could have led to my downfall, thankfully nothing of the sort ever happened. Given that, having gone through the same torment again and again; writing, drafting, editing, and proofreading the manuscript was nothing less than mentally exhausting.

In no way do I mean this piece of fiction would change society, but more so to highlight the way young girls are perceived in society. How we are so quick to judge anyone based on one aspect of them that is alien to us. Conversely, the same stands true in the other sense too, for women who put allegations against a male, are readily accepted, without taking the pain of going into the depths, just because the face value of it is believable.

I admit to being one of the 'quick to judge' lot until I become a victim of it. What changed was really after attending college, meeting people with diverse backgrounds, having different goals and aspirations, exploring different sexualities, etc. really helped me broaden my perspective on life and be more accepting of differences, which I couldn't have achieved by staying in my very comfortable hometown. It really is this time you give yourself that you finally grow up!

Share Your Love

If you have arrived at this part of the book, I have the deepest gratitude for you, and I would love to know your most candid and genuine thoughts about it to improve and grow my craft!

'You Were Always There' is my second standalone book.

You can also read my first book of a trilogy, Telekinesis Vol. 1: Victims of His Head.

An exclusive excerpt of 'Telekinesis Vol. 1: Victims of His Head by Devleena' is attached at the end of the novel.

I am also open to taking in personal stories and memoirs from individuals who want their stories to be presented to the world, as either a biography or a piece of fiction.

Write to me at dv.yourssincerely@gmail.com

If you like my book, leave a review of the book on the Amazon / Goodreads link of 'You Were Always There by Devleena Naik', you can also tag or follow me on Instagram for more updates on my upcoming novels - @devleenanaik @dv_purplesun.

Order an exclusive Author's signed copy gift box for your loved ones. Just email me at dv.yourssincerely@gmail.com with your name and the person you want to send this gift to!

An exclusive extract from Devleena Naik's first novel

TELEKINESIS
Vol. 1
VICTIMS OF HIS HEAD

Reader's Discretion is advised

Follow @dv_purplesun for live updates

"I got off at the transit station and waited for the next bus. The bus took quite a while to arrive, but fortunately, I had some extra time today. When I boarded the bus, there were only ten other passengers: three lively 15-something-year-old girls, an elderly lady, and the ticket collector. I walked past them and took a seat in the second-to-last row. I plugged in my headphones to fully enjoy the suburban view."

Now that I have all the time to think (20 minutes, to be precise).

The Reason by Hoobastank it is.

"There are many things I wish I didn't do, but I continue learning..."

I shouldn't have said those things to her. Maybe we really need a fresh start. I'm not a perfect person; it's true. She deserved better. The best she did all this while was just to be herself. She could have played the imposter and tried to be Io, but she didn't. I was not the best sister either.

As I stepped onto the bus, the old lady got off while a few others boarded, including some girls from my college. Ugh, those girls are so annoying. I really wish I could adopt their carefree, impassive attitude and strut through life as they do.

At the next stop, a guy walked in and asked if he could take the seat beside me.

"Of course," I said, trying to act nonchalant.

It's not like I really care; the seat was empty anyway. Maybe I was better off not sharing my space with anyone.

Wait, did I say that too loudly? Darn, these headphones!

It's not that I'm not interested in boys. I find them attractive, but I don't think I am emotionally capable of engaging in a conversation without making myself look foolish.

Anyway, I look outside the window. We reach the outskirts of the city, and I see kids playing joyfully amongst themselves, their laughter resonating through the air, while towering trees reach up towards the endless sky, creating a breathtaking natural canopy. The views from where I stand are nothing short of amazing, filling me with a sense of peace and wonder.

But...

Wait. What place is this? This is not my usual route. Did I board the wrong bus?

I turn to look inside for the conductor, and.........

FU**KKKKK!!!

I see the conductor's face a few feet away from mine, shouting, "Surrender your phones, and any smart move will be your end!"

The bus has been hijacked. The driver calls him out! 'Souvik!!'

The conductor approached him and handed over a jute bag. He took away our phones and other belongings and put them in the bag near the door to keep them out of reach. While on the way, they stopped at a desolate place and threw all the phones into the sewage drain. Then, at intervals and varying distances, they discarded our belongings.

I am freaking out. Where am I? What did I just do? This is the wrong bus, oh my God!! What is happening?

I see all the people on the bus screaming for help! I stand there still with my hands behind my back! I see a girl taking out some of the hair accessories tied on her head to attack the conductor, but the driver sees her and shouts, "Souvik, look out, the girl behind you!!"

Souvik runs up to her and catches her head. His face turns red, and he snatches it off her head to throw it away. He then starts screaming like a madman, pulls out a gun and shoots her!

...

There is dead-drop silence. No one dares to move an ounce.

"We have dealt with fools like you before. You move, you die. You all are now the offerings to our God!" Souvik declares.

WHAT ON EARTH WAS THAT!?

Have I seen death with my naked eye? My heart starts pounding; my body is shivering with fear... but not as much that can catch the eye of the heartless man in front of me... Who are these people, and why are they even doing this!!! What is this? There's blood all over the place. And what God? What is this cult!? Is this a joke? A religious sacrifice? Political propaganda? What did we do? Why us? What is wrong with these people? I need to think of some way to flee.

He takes the girl's corpse to the front of the bus and wraps it up in rugs. They barely wipe the blood off the floor and throw out the body in the next sewage.

I have never seen such insanity in the name of sacrifice! The girl was protecting herself! Who are these monsters? I can't stay like this, but moving even an inch could be fatal; they can kill us all. I need to go home!!

He asks us all to sit and ties our hands to the seat in front. Then, he takes out a jar with pills and a bottle of some fluid. They look like sedatives.

"Take these like good boys or you die," he goes up to the guy in the first seat.

His eyes express desperate refusal, but he begs him to spare his life.

We have nothing to contact anyone around. How will we ever get out of here?

Souvik forcibly opens that guy's mouth and gives him the pill. He gasps into the ground, coughing and choking. Souvik then grabs his neck, pulls him close to pour the fluid inside his mouth, and jerks him back to his seat. The boy's body turns pale, and he coughs for some time, and then he faints.

"If you people don't want bad fortune upon yourself, then do as I saw, for as long as you follow me, you stay alive! The moment you don't, you just set an example for the rest!" He threatens.

He walks up to everyone seat by seat and passes on the pill. Nobody dares to revolt.

There are twelve girls and six boys alive on the bus. Our hearts were hammering our chests as we struggled against the restraints. Fear had consumed us.

He comes up to me, and I obediently take the pill with the fluid, avoiding any eye contact with him. I feel my body heating up almost instantly after taking it. My legs start to hurt, and I fall back to my seat. I felt a similar twisting of the stomach as last night; this is just worse. My forehead started sweating, and I could not hold back my tears. All my life flashes before my eyes, and my head starts to feel heavy...

All this pain continues for three minutes straight until I pass out...

***

Disclaimer: Reader's Discretion

This book is not meant for a universal audience, as there are certain sensitive subjects explored, which include:

1. Mental Health: Erotomania and Delusions
2. Stalking
3. Cyberbullying
4. Use of Strong Language

Kindly refer to this before reading the no

vel.